Michael Gregory II

New Witch in Town

This book is dedicated to my wife and family. You have always been my motivation to do better.

chapter 1

Have you ever seen a woman that you don't understand why, but you can't take your eyes away from her? You look around and everyone else is doing the same thing. Men, women, children, and even animals alike can't seem to take their eyes off this particular woman. They are rare beings; it is rare you can encounter such a divine specimen. In the times there is one of these special feminine spectacles, they carry with them an ability to dictate their surroundings. How a person in power can command their subordinates, except these women can do it with anyone or anything.

One of these creatures has entered our town of Forestdale and believe me, every single person has noticed. She's a mystery, one that many want to solve. She has been the talk of our little town. No one knows her name, but everyone wants to. Everyone is creating stories about her as if they know anything when they have no idea. Here is what I do know. She's got platinum blonde hair that goes halfway down her back and flows in the wind, yet sets perfectly styled afterward. She has stunning almond-shaped green eyes that when you look into them, even for a second, you feel as if you've been taken into a trance. She is around five foot four, slender, and with a little curve in the right areas. She tends to wear black mini dresses or skirts often that are tight and hug her body as if it was just a second part of her skin. She's pale in tone, yet you can tell she has a slight tan. All the men dream of her. The women are envious or secretly lusting for her and try to disguise it by gossiping about her and spreading rumors.

The one thing that I have noticed is there is a glowing aura about her, something you cannot explain. This, I believe, is the reason everyone is scared to talk to her. I am not sure if anyone even knows where she lives or when she even arrived here. She goes to the grocery store to gather fruits, vegetables, herbs, and meat. Occasionally, she will go to the local nursery and get several plants that she loads into the back of her jeep and ride off into the distance, where she disappears on the horizon. Come to think of it, I'm not even sure if the cashiers even exchange any words with her besides what is owed. Does she talk to them? Does she say anything at all? I wonder what her voice sounds like; I bet it is soft and beautiful. I have an intense draw to her; I don't know why, but I must get to know her. I want to know everything about her. I guess there are a lot of others that probably want to do the same in this town. But it will be I, Mark Granger, who will get to know this mystery woman.

Let me introduce myself. I have lived in

Forestdale my whole life. I am twenty-three years old and have lived in the same house since I was born with my mother and sister. They have both moved out since and have gotten their own places. They didn't like to still live in that house ever since the accident. My father had passed away when I was a young child in an accident at his work where he had fallen off of a building, but his coworkers did not have him strapped into the safety harness like he was supposed to be. For that reason, my family hasn't had to work due to the large payouts from life insurance and from the company for not following safety protocols. I am considered an oddball in town, an outcast. Maybe that is the reason I am drawn to this outsider that has entered our small town. There is something special about a person who shakes up a whole town just by their sheer presence. We have been blessed with one of those special people. I must get to know her.

chapter **2**

spend most days in town driving around, thinking about this mystery woman. Wondering if I will get a sighting of her, wondering when is the next time she comes for necessities? Will I be near? It might sound a little obsessive, but it truly is just that. I have a want, a need, to find who this person is and why I am so intrigued by her. I also want to see all the townsfolk squirm, knowing that I did the one thing they all wanted to do but was too scared to do so.

Then there it is. I see her black jeep driving down the road. It appears to be heading straight towards me. I am at the grocery store, buying my normal daily nibbles: an energy drink, beef jerky, and a string cheese. Does a body good. Shit! What do I do? I need to prepare myself and not make it look like I am trying to set this meeting up. It needs to be organic, or at least appear to be. Looks like I will be doing some extra grocery shopping today. Time to go inside and grab a cart. Time to buy groceries for the week, for the second time. Keep it together Mark, you are just here shopping for groceries, nothing else. At least make it seem that way. Right now you are talking to yourself too much.

There she is, getting out of her Jeep. She looks gorgeous. Wearing black stretch pants that hug her body so well that it could pass off as painted skin. She's wearing this black t-shirt with some sort of design on it, looks like moon cycles. The way she steps out of her Jeep with the wind blowing in her hair is mesmerizing. It's almost as if time has slowed down and everyone stopped to watch the new movie that is our stranger here in Forestdale.

I am walking around grabbing things nonchalant, pretending to be really into the food items that are in front of me. Let's go to the produce. I know I can run into her there. Will I be able to muster up the courage to actually speak with her though? That is the real question. Hopefully, all will go according to plan and I will finally be the first person to converse with her directly, maybe even become friends? Alright, focus. Let's look at this watermelon. Pick it up, tap it, thud thud, ok not a good one. Needs to sound hollow. Pick up another, dink dink, ok, this one sounds good. I look around and oh shit, she's right in front of me. Don't panic, she is looking at me, smiling.

The mystery girl says to me, "sounds like you got a winner."

I respond, "Yeah, sounds like it. I love watermelon, so I bet this will be a good one." Fuck, she's talking to me. Holy shit, it worked. Don't panic, act natural. "You're new in town.

How do you like it?"

"It's nice here, peaceful. Suits my needs."

"It is definitely quiet. My name is Mark, Mark Granger. Welcome to Forestdale. What is your name, if you don't mind me asking?"

"Thanks, my name is Marie."

"Well, it's nice to meet you, Marie. Have you met many people in town yet?"

"No, in fact, you're the first one I've actually had a conversation with. Most people around seem to be shy."

"Yea, the townsfolk here are very shy. When a new person comes into town, everyone seems to notice, but everyone is kind of scaredy cats when it comes to talking to new people. Especially when they look like you." Shit, why did I say that?

Marie slightly grins on one side of her mouth. "That's ok, I am glad that I finally got to talk to someone, and that the someone be you."

"I am also glad I got to meet and speak to you finally as well." Mark dammit, you keep saying too much. Shut your mouth. "Hey, hopefully this isn't too forward, but I would love for you to come share this watermelon with me sometime."

"Ok, I would love to. It would be nice to sit down and spend time with something that is human."

"Great, how about tomorrow at two pm?" Did she say something that is human?

"Sounds good."

"I live at the big house on the corner across from Forestdale elementary. Do you know where that is?"

"Yes, I do. I will see you tomorrow at two pm."

Marie then walked away with a smirk on her face.

I did it, I actually did it. I spoke with her. I found out her name. Oh my god, I set up a get together with her tomorrow. Is it a date? No, I didn't say a date. Does she think it's a date? Oh no, what do I do? I need to set up my house and make it presentable. Should we eat it outside? Inside? Should I make lunch with candle light?

What should I pair up with watermelon? Think Mark, what have you gotten yourself in to? This is exactly what you wanted, but you didn't think that this would actually happen. Ok, I got an idea. Let's get another watermelon. I can make a watermelon lemonade to pair up with the cut slices of watermelon. Then I can get a bunch of meats and cheeses with crackers. I can make one of those charcuterie boards. Yea, this works. Oh, then I can have a secondary board with all fruits. Already have the watermelon. I know, cherries, blueberries, raspberries, tangerines, nectarines, peaches, perfect. Oh, I know, I should get some bourbon, and vodka, maybe some tequila, in case she wants to spike her watermelon lemonade she has options. Can't forget the mint.

Now what do I do? I feel like I have to do so much. First, I need to look presentable, not desperate. Haircut and a shave, yes. What time is it? Three pm, ok, the barber is still open. Better hurry and get that done. After, rush home and clean up any messes that are around the house. Clean up the backyard in case she wants to be out there. Oh yea, can't forget to play with my dog Ginger. Dinner, can't forget to eat dinner. Ok it all sounds good to me.

After standing there in the grocery store going over all the things I need to do to prepare in my head, I look up and notice everyone is staring at me. Some are grinning, mostly the men. The others have a look of concern, mostly the women. I look out the large glass windows and notice her jeep was gone. At that moment, several people came up to me, all asking the same questions, and fast. "What did you talk to her about?" "What did she say?" "Did she cast a spell on you?" "Did she ask you for money?" "She looks like bad news; you better watch out." 'Did you get her number?"

I raise my arms and respond, slightly irritated, "Calm down everyone. She's a nice girl. It just so happens I will be meeting up with her tomorrow to eat some watermelon and conversate. Keep all your judgements to yourself. There's nothing more to it than just a couple of adults getting together for friendly conversation. Now go about your day."

Everyone looks shocked. At that point, everyone is walking away. Some of the elderly women I could hear murmuring grumpily, "I bet she's going to take his soul or rob him at least. Poor boy doesn't know what the succubus will do to him."

I now realize how much my town was full of insecure, judge mental people who did not like anyone out of what they would consider the norm. Good thing I fit that same criterion, so it makes me feel even better about meeting Marie. I still can't believe I got her name, even better that we are getting together tomorrow. Oh Marie, how I cannot wait to finally get together and find out everything there is to find out about you. Shit! Tomorrow! I better hurry. I am daydreaming too much already and it's setting me back. The crazy thing is, I think I am in love and I have only met her once and barely found out her name. I cannot wait till tomorrow!

Chapter 3

t is almost two o'clock in the afternoon and I don't even feel close to being ready for Marie to be here. I at least have all the fruits cut up and placed. I have the meat boards set up. Berries, I need to place the berries and make it look more colorful. Watermelon is cut into triangle pieces. I have also made watermelon lemonade; I hope she wants to mix it with her bourbon. Ok, time to set out all the boards on the table in the backyard. Bring out the tea, grab the bottles of bourbon, tequila, vodka, beer. Have to make sure she has all the different options. Well, I guess this is as good as it can get. Oh no, I need to take a shower! I smell like a dirty armpit.

I rush upstairs and jump in the shower. No time to shave, just a quick wash. Jump out of the shower, look for clean clothes. What should I wear? I will wear my black jeans and a dark button-up shirt. Seems fitting seeing that she normally wears black always. So I want to make sure I fit in with what would make her comfortable. Ok, deodorant, brush teeth, cologne, brush hair, part to the side, good to go. Just in time, I hear the doorbell ring and the dog starts barking. Don't freak out, try to act natural when opening the door.

I open the door and there she is. Looking oh so stunning with a black tight mini dress, low cut. Black converse shoes with black ankle socks. She is holding a bottle of some sorts.

I say to her, "Hi Marie, welcome to my humble abode. How are you doing today?"

She responds, "Mark, I am good. I brought you some bourbon that I made myself."

"Wow, that's amazing. Please come on in. I can't wait to taste your bourbon. I forgot. I hope you're not allergic to dogs or cats. I have both in here somewhere."

"Nope, not allergic. I love animals. I can't wait to meet them."

At that moment, I hear Ginger, my German Shepherd, going nuts in the backyard, clawing at the back door, trying to get in. Not realizing that the door was slightly cracked, Ginger manages to open the door and comes barreling in like there was a giant pile of peanut butter that I was stashing sitting on the floor. She comes running straight for Marie. In a panic I try to stop her but she had already run past me. The odd thing is, as soon as she gets to Marie, she stops and sits quietly at attention.

"Ginger, what are you doing? Don't bother Marie. I am so sorry; she normally doesn't do things like that."

"It's totally ok. Like I said, I love animals. They love me too."

"I can see that. Ginger normally at least

jumps on anyone that comes over."

"Ginger is a good girl, aren't you?" Marie said in a cute baby talk like voice.

At that moment, I knew there was something special about her. I knew there was more than meets the eye. She got the obedience of Ginger when she barely gets that from me after all the years of training.

At that moment, Marie looks at me, smiles and asks, "So where can I put this bourbon?"

"I am so sorry. I got distracted. Let me take it and put it with the other bottles in the back."

"Sounds good. Let's get this party started."

"Yes, let's."

I take her to the backyard and set her homemade bourbon with the other bottles. This bottle catches my eye after I set it down. It has an appearance of something that could be really old. It looks like it has some sort of drawings or symbols on it, but it's hard to tell with the darkness of the whiskey. I look up, hoping I wasn't staring at the bottle too long and making myself look even more like an idiot. There is

Marie, standing just about a foot and a half away from me with a big grin and says, "so...... you ready to try it? I made it intentionally for you. It should go great with your watermelon lemonade you made."

"Ok." I responded. "Sounds amazing, I love all things bourbon, especially one that can be mixed with watermelon lemonade. Hey did you say you made it intentionally for me? Doesn't that take a long time to make?"

"Yes silly. I didn't mean I made it for you. I meant I was bottling it for you while thinking about you this morning. It takes a minimum of two years to make bourbon. Wouldn't that be absurd if I could just wave my hand and say some words and presto, there you have some bourbon?"

The one thing that caught me off guard after she had said this, she said it with a huge grin on her face. Then she winked at me, making an exaggerated winking face as if she was saying just kidding. I don't know whether to be frightened or excited by this. Well, I guess the only rational thing to do right now would be to start drinking the bourbon and get these conversations going. I grab two glasses, fill up with some ice, add in the bourbon, about a shot worth. Throw in the cherries that have been cut in half and squeeze some of the juice in there. Now, for the final touch, add in the watermelon lemonade and now we have ourselves the solution to have a good time.

"So Marie, where are you from? What brought you to this little town?"

"Oh, I am from neither here nor there. I am kind of from everywhere. I stopped in this city because something smelled yummy. I had to find out what it was."

"Ooook. I am not really sure what you mean by that. You didn't grow up in one town? Oh, I get it. You moved around a lot. "

"Yea, you can say that."

"Well...... Did you ever find that yummy smell? I guess what I am asking is if you found what you were looking for?"

"I haven't quite found it yet. I think I am

getting close to it though. I think it's possible it might even be near me right now."

"Oh nice, maybe it's the watermelon cocktail I made."

"Maybe." Marie responded with a seductive smile.

Dammit Mark, why did you say that? You are making yourself look foolish again. Sometimes I wish I could just say things in a way that they don't seem so ridiculous.

"Ok, Marie. It's time to have another drink and let's get to the snacking. I set out all these boards with fruits, cheeses, meats. Pretty much everything because I wasn't sure what you would want or like. Sound good?"

"Sounds good to me, Mark. I love snacking. I love food in general."

"By the way, Marie, this bourbon is amazing. I love bourbon and that's what I pretty much drink exclusively. I must say that this one is really hitting the spot. How long have you been making bourbon for yourself?"

"Thank you. I have been making it for what

seems like one hundred years. It's an old family recipe that's been handed down for generations. "

"It truly is amazing. You should sell it. Make a lot of it and sell it worldwide. I'm telling you; you would have a fortune."

"This is a special recipe to us. We will never sell it. We only drink it with special people, other than our family members, of course."

"Wow, I feel honored. I hope I didn't offend you by saying you should sell it. I understand not wanting to give out your secrets."

"You're too serious Mark Granger." Marie said with a chuckle. "I am not offended. I have too many secrets that I won't give out. If you're lucky, I will let you in on some."

"If I could only be so lucky."

Now that the bourbon is settling in, I am feeling a little looser. Marie seems to be getting relaxed as well. This is going much better than I thought. I knew she would be a nice girl. There was more than meets the eye with her. I am even more intrigued by her. There is something so magnetizing about her. Every second we spend together; I feel as if I am being drawn closer and closer. I swear it's not only because she is so beautiful on the outside. That alone is distracting. There is something else about her though. I need to know more about her. I hope I can keep this going and don't scare her off.

"So, Marie, tell me a little about yourself."

"Ok Mark, ask me questions. What do you want to know? Don't worry, I don't scare off easily."

That was weird. Why did she say it like that? Did she just read my mind? No, I am sure it was just a coincidence.

"Ok, let's see. I got it. Let's go over some basics to kick off the day. What's your favorite color?"

"Oooh fun, my favorite color is periwinkle. What's yours?"

"Hey now, I am the one asking questions. You can have your turn afterwards. Mine is red and black. What's your favorite food?"

"Sir yes sir! My favorite food is steak, bloody.

Throw in some greens or broccoli with it."

"Wow, this bourbon is strong. I wasn't expecting to get wasted so early in the day. Oh well, I guess that just means we have that much more time to spend together, doesn't it?"

"I guess you're right, aren't you? I am waiting for another question though."

"Ok, let's see. What's your favorite drink?"

"You're having it right now."

"Nice, I understand why. This is delicious. I feel like I can drink this forever. It's hot out here. Do you want to go swimming?"

"It is hot. I would love to go swimming. But I didn't know I was supposed to bring a swimsuit."

"Oh shit, I completely forgot to tell you to bring one if you wanted to. I didn't even think about swimming till now. Sorry about that, maybe next time."

"I didn't say that changes anything. I still want to go swimming. I hope you don't mind me going swimming in my underwear."

"I don't mind at all."

"I hope you plan on swimming in your

underwear to make it even."

"Alright, fuck it. Let's do this. First, let's take a shot of your amazing bourbon."

We grab the bottle of bourbon, and I grab two of the boards with the meats and fruits so we can snack at the same time. We now walk over to where the pool is and set everything down. Marie takes a swig from the bottle because we didn't bring shot glasses. She hands it to me and says, "bottoms up." I take a swig and continue to feel better and better. Now it's time to get ready to swim. I look over at her and she takes off her shoes and I follow her lead in doing the same. Now the socks have been removed. She looks at me with a big smile, then winks and pulls her mini dress up and over her head to take it off. I pause in awe when I see the sheer beauty of her amazing body. She's, of course, wearing a black bra and a black thong. I'm drunk at this point so I couldn't help but sit and stare. She turned around and ran and dove into the pool.

"Are you just going to stand there, or are you coming in too?" Marie shouts.

"Yup, coming right in." I replied.

I rip off my shirt and pull off my pants as fast as I can. Hopefully, I didn't look too excited. I run and cannonball into the water. We then swim and continue to chat while snacking and taking shots every so often. Time passes on and next thing we know, it's already six o'clock. I ask if she wants to get out of the pool now and she agrees. As she gets out, I hold the towel up for her. I wrap it around her while doing my best to not stare at her amazing body. This has been such an amazing time. I don't even know how to express the fun I have had with this person who I only met yesterday. The funny thing is, it feels as if we have actually known each other our whole lives. The way we connect and click with each other. I can only describe it as incredible. I don't want this day to end. I don't want our time together to end. We must do this again.

I start to say, "Marie, I think—"

Marie interrupts me and says, "We should definitely do this again. We can get together and swim or eat, or whatever else you want to do. I had a lot of fun with you, Mark. I haven't had this much fun in a long time."

"Neither have I Marie. This has been amazing."

Marie then drops her towel with a big smile on her face. She turns around, knowing that I will stare at her as she walks away to get her clothes and put them back on. I think I am in love. How can this be? I just met her. I don't know a lot about her. She even said she has many secrets. Ones that she won't tell me, or at least not yet. There is a certain comfortability I have with her though. One that cannot be explained. I remember she has put on her clothes while I am still just sitting here staring at her and am still in my underwear. Shit, that's embarrassing. I hurry and throw my jeans on so I can walk her out.

"So Marie, how can I get ahold of you so we can plan the next time we get together?"

"Give me your number and I will get a hold of you. Just so you know, it will be random and I will want you to drop what you're doing so we can do something spur of the moment. Are you ok with that?"

"Fuck it, why not? I could always have some more spontaneity in my life."

At this moment I hear my front door open fast and furiously. I know it could only mean one thing. My idiot friend Braden came over uninvited, like he usually does. Of course, he would choose the absolute worst time to come over.

"Sounds like my friend has made his way over. That's not the spontaneity I was looking forward to." I say with a laugh. "Let me walk you to the door. Are you going to be able to drive? Do you need an uber or anything to get home?"

"I have a high tolerance; I will be just fine. Besides, I stopped drinking a while ago, even though you kept going. I ate a lot of the yummy food too, so it helped. Thanks though."

"No problem at all. Thanks again for the fun time. I am looking forward to hearing from you soon."

I then walk Marie to the front door to see her

off. Half way there we hear in the distance. "Hey fuck face. Where are you?"

I yell back, "I'll be right there Braden."

Hoping I can get her to her car before they cross paths. No luck. We run directly into him.

Braden says, "Whoa, Mark. Sorry, I didn't realize you had such beautiful company over "

"Maybe you should've called like a normal person." I reply agitatedly.

Ignoring me, Braden looks Marie up and down and says, "Hello beautiful. My name is Braden. I promise you will like me so much more. And what might your name be?"

Marie replies with a fierce attitude, "Just leaving. I am feeling a little overcrowded now."

"Ouch." Said Braden.

"Bye Mark. Thank you for the amazing time. I will talk to you soon. Have a good rest of your night,"

"Bye. Same for me. Have a great night and I am looking forward to hearing from you."

Just like that, she walked out of the door and she was gone. I look over and I see Braden staring at me with the biggest grin I have seen on his face.

chapter 4

Braden was staring at me with his devilish grin. I knew he was about to ask me something obnoxious, so I just stared back at him with a very annoyed look on my face.

"What is it Braden?"

"Who was that? Why did I not know anything about this? There are so many questions I have. What the fuck Mark, where was my invite?"

"There was a reason I didn't tell your stupid ass. You would've come over and ruined everything like you almost did right now."

"Well, that's not very nice. It's not like she's your girlfriend or anything. I would've liked to get to know this mystery girl that no one knows about around town. How did you pull it off to have her come over here?"

"I ran into her at the store and asked her if she wanted to come over and talk over some watermelon lemonade."

"Why are you shirtless? Why are you wet? I smell booze on you too. Are you drunk?"

"One thing led to another. We were drinking and went swimming in our underwear. But that is all I am going to tell you. Don't ask me any pervy questions that I know you are going to have."

"Well, that's no fun. I never realized how hot she was."

"Anyway Braden, why did you come over?"

"It was the talk of the town. I heard you were going to be meeting up with her. Remember, you told everyone in the store after you made plans?"

Well, I guess he is right on that one. I let everyone know what I was going to do with her. I shouldn't have said anything. Oh well, it all worked out.

"Yea, I guess you're right on that one. Anyway, I am really fucked up right now. Do you have anything important to say? I want to enjoy my drunkenness."

"Buzzkill, ok fine. You don't have to convince me; I will gladly drink with you."

"Wait what? I didn't say that. I said I wanted time alone."

"Come on. Did you get to see her naked? Did you kiss her? What did you guys do? Come on, man, how good did she look swimming?"

"Again, Braden, I don't want to answer your pervy questions. I just want to enjoy myself. I had an amazing day with her. We ate food. We drank booze. We went swimming in our underwear. That's it. Now let me go back and start drinking and snacking more."

"Hold up. You went swimming in your underwear? Does she wear underwear? Did she skinny dip? Oh my god, I bet she was stunning. Did you sneak any pictures of her? It's ok buddy, you can show me I won't say anything."

"Fuck you Braden. Not everyone thinks that way. I just had fun with her. No pictures. No skinny dipping."

At this point Braden had already grabbed himself a glass of the bourbon I had set out. Immediately, I realize Marie had left her bottle of homemade bourbon on my table. I am going to grab that nonchalant so Braden doesn't notice. I grabbed it and took it to the living room, where I could hide it behind one of the pillows. I don't want him to try her family's special recipe.

"That's it Mark, we are going to sit here and get drunk as fuck. We won't stop until you spill all the beans on this one." Braden demanded.

"Braden, I mean this will all sincerity. Fuck you. I will not tell you shit. I am already drunk. In fact, I might just pass out if I keep going. So why don't you politely go fuck yourself?"

"Damn Mark, you are drunk. You don't have to be such an asshole though. I just want to know about the new girl. She looks really hot. She's got that sexy, mysterious flavor too."

"No shit Braden. Why the fuck do you think I was talking to her in the first place? She's gorgeous. When you talk to her, you fall even more for her because she's awesome."

"Oh, I get it now. You have feelings for this one, don't you? I can tell you're acting different with this one."

"I only just met her. If I am being honest, though, I am really attracted to her."

"Perfect. I am going to try to seduce her then."

"What the fuck Braden?"

"That's right. I can't have my friend get to the new girl before me. She's hot, and I bet she's into some kinky shit."

"Seriously Braden, fuck you. Get out of my house. Don't disrespect me and don't disrespect Marie."

"There it is. Her name is Marie. I will fuck Marie before you are even a thought."

At that point, I am livid and have a lot of

liquid courage. I stood up angrily, walked over, and punched him right in the face. He fell back and tripped over the couch. I grabbed him by the shirt and pulled him to throw him out of my front door. He pulled away from me and pushed me.

"Mark, you fucked up. You're a dick. You never should've hit me. I will make you regret this."

"Fuck you Braden. Maybe you should think about others for once. Don't be such a disrespectful bitch, especially to your supposed friends."

Braden walked out of the front door and slammed it on his way out. I could hear him yelling some sort of obscenities before peeling out in his car as he left. There is no doubt this is going to cause some sort of backlash. Braden isn't one to let bygones be bygones.

chapter 5

Traveling into town, I am already feeling nervous about what repercussions are going to ensue from standing up to Braden yesterday. He is a vengeful bastard. He has never been one to let things go. Especially if someone got the better of him. I, on the other hand, made him look like a fool. I also assaulted him, which was a double whammy. One thing that might be in my favor, no one else was there to witness it.

Braden works in town as the local butcher. So there will be no avoiding him. There will be no other alternative. I guess the only way would be to go vegan or vegetarian. That sure as hell will not happen. So I guess I need to try to make amends or something. I just don't know how I am going to do it. We have had many disagreements in the past and have made up; I guess. The only thing is there has always been an elephant in the room, something that makes the friendship not exactly a normal one. There is always that competitiveness and his want to be in control; to be the better. This is the first time that a woman has been the wedge. This time, it felt different. It felt personal.

I pulled up to the store. I really don't want to get out of my car. Something feels off. I need to get some things though. I need to load up on some steaks and meats. So there will definitely be no avoiding him. Alright Mark, here we go. Grab a cart, walk to the back of the store. There is the butcher's counter. No one is there. Maybe he called in sick today, or maybe it was his day off. I could only be so lucky. I ring the bell at the counter, waiting for someone to help, and

Braden walks through the back door. He has a smile on his face. He also has a black eye. I feel like all the blood drained out of my head and dropped to my feet. I didn't know what to expect.

"Hey Mark, what's up? What can I get for you?" Braden said in a friendly matter.

"Oh, hey Braden. I need ten pounds of rib eyes, five pounds of ground beef, and let's do three racks of ribs. How are you doing?" I responded questionably.

"Ok Mark, sounds good. I will grab all that stuff right now. I am good. Just staying busy. How are you?"

"I am good. Look, about last night."

"Don't worry about it Mark, I know I went too far, and I was an asshole. Let's not mention this ever again, cool?"

"Ok, sounds good. I am sorry for my part too. I was drunk and things went too far."

"Mark, like I said. Let's just not mention it ever again. I am going to get your meat now."

Braden walked to the back to go cut all the

meat I asked for. Something felt really off about the whole situation. This was too easy. Nothing with Braden could be that easy. So I will still stay on high alert. As I was standing at the counter, there were others walking behind me. I was just minding my own business until I saw out of the corner of my eye that some townies were staring at me when they walked by. I decided I would turn around and look at everyone to see if I was just thinking things that weren't actually there. Nope. They are staring at me. Some are even shaking their heads. This is odd.

"Hey, why are you shaking your head at me?" I yelled at a man as he walked by. "You lady, what's your problem?"

The man turned around and walked up to me and replied, "It's a real shame you could allow something to happen like that to your best friend."

"What are you talking about?"

"Well, Braden told us what happened at your house last night. How that evil woman came over to your house and attacked him for no reason other than she thought it would be funny."

"You have got to be fucking kidding me. That didn't happen at all. She is a good person. She didn't even hit him."

"Then how would you explain Braden's black eye? I am just going to walk off now so I don't embarrass him when he comes out. Maybe you should get some manners and teach your new pet to have them too."

I am fucking livid. How could he lie about this? Why did he just tell me how he didn't want to mention any of it? I do not know what to think right now. Just then Braden walked out from the back with all of my cuts.

"Here you go Mark, and don't worry. I marked down all the prices for a friend discount."

"Why did you lie Braden? All these people have some false story that Marie hit you for fun."

"Well, I had to tell them something about why I have a black eye. I was trying to protect you. If I said it was you, you wouldn't be able to come in and get any more meat."

"But that's not what happened. You started it all. You said ridiculous shit to me. Of course I was going to fucking hit you. I am feeling like doing it again right now."

"Uh, Mark. You are making a scene. Can you please just grab your stuff and go home and get sleep? I got this."

"Why don't you just tell the fucking truth? Tell everyone what really fucking happened."

"Ok Mark. You have to just grab your stuff and go now. You don't want to get banned from here."

"This isn't over, Braden. This is just wrong."

I grabbed all of my beef, threw them into my shopping cart, and walked away as fast as I can. I got to the register and noticed everyone staring again. This time I am just mad.

"Everyone, stop staring at me. The story you heard from Braden is not true. He is a mother fucking liar."

Everyone just kind of gasped or made some sort of rude breathing gesture, implying they didn't believe me. Whatever. These people are all idiots anyway. Braden was obviously playing games with me. Trying to turn the whole town onto Marie. Outcast her even more than she already is. What a real dick move on his part. I guess that is all a part of his game though. The one where he tries to make me suffer. Why? I don't really know. Some sort of friend, huh? The sad part is he knows how to play the game and manipulate all the surrounding people. Now it's not just me he's making suffer though, he is putting shit onto Marie. That is where I draw the line. I need to figure out what I can do to make sure this all goes away. I need to do something about Braden; he has messed with my life for the last time.

chapter 6

After the fiasco that happened in the store, I was livid. I didn't know what to do. I drove home as fast as I could. I just wanted to get home and forget that had ever happened. Forget that Braden once again is fucking up my life. When I pulled up to my house and the first thing I notice is a black Jeep in my driveway. No way, Marie's back. She came back. I didn't think I would see her again after last night. She's sitting on my porch with Ginger. How did Ginger get out? Well, at least Ginger likes Marie. I guess that makes two of us.

"Hi Marie, how are you doing?"

"Hi Mark, I am good. Even better that I got to hang out with Ginger here."

"Yea, she's an amazing dog. She always makes for good company. Hey, how did she get out of the backyard?"

"I hope it's ok, but I let her out. She was whining and digging at the side gate. So, I figured I would let her out and hang out with her, giving her all the pets and scratches she could handle while waiting for you to get home."

"Actually, that's great. She loves getting all the attention she can get....I wasn't sure if I was going to see you again after last night. Sorry about that. Braden is a complete dickhead."

"Why wouldn't you see me again? You did nothing wrong. Besides Braden, I had a blast and would love to do it again. Also, you're kind of the only person I know and talk to in this town."

"Well, when you put it that way, I guess you have no choice but to talk to me, do you?" I say with a sly smirk and a chuckle.

"Well, don't go getting all full of yourself now. I might just have to call you Braden."

"Ouch."

The flirting was nice. There was some real chemistry between us, I could feel it. I mean, I always felt a natural draw to her. As if there were some sort of interdimensional magnets that we couldn't see, but they were pulling us together. Well, at least they were pulling me towards her. I know everyone in town had some sort of magnetism towards her, but I know mine was different.

"So, speaking of Braden, there's actually something important that I need to talk to you about. Let's go inside. I'll get us some drinks ready."

"Uh oh, someone's in trouble." Marie says jokingly as she stands up and casually walks to the front door. I grab my groceries and open up the front door while Ginger was waiting patiently sitting next to Marie. She really does like her; she never acts this way with people. I put away all the meat, stashed some in the freezer and some in the fridge for the next day or two. I grab some bourbon, wishing she had brought her family recipe bottle again. Right before I pour it, Marie wiggles her index finger while making a "Tsk, tsk, tsk." I smile and wonder at the same time, did she just read my mind? She smiles even bigger after I thought that. Ok, that's weird, but I won't think too much of it. I grab the bottle from her and while pouring our drinks I say "Now that's what I was hoping for. This bourbon is seriously the best I've ever had."

"Thanks. I had a feeling it would disappoint you if I didn't bring it."

"I most definitely would have been. I am going to need to get a bottle or two from you one day so I could always have it on hand."

"Wouldn't you like that?" Marie responds flirtatiously.

"I most definitely would. Ok. So the thing that I wanted to talk to you about. Braden, he spread rumors around the town. He told everyone you gave him a black eye and attacked him last night."

"What, why? Why does he have a black eye?"

"I hit him last night. He was being even more of a dick. He is telling stories to get back at me. I think it's because... well, because I like you. I think he wants to ruin that like he always tries to ruin everything for me."

"I like you too. You're so nice. Well, thanks for telling me, so I will know why people look at me funny when I go back to town. I don't really care though. So they can think what they want. I might just make some fun out of it and startle people by throwing my hands up at them and yelling obscenities to make them think I am really crazy."

"That's definitely one way to handle it. Quite hilarious too. I would love to see that, actually."

"Next time I go into town, I'll stop by and pick you up then so you can have a free show."

"Deal. Now enough of that. Let's focus on this bourbon. Do you want to play a game of pool?"

"Sounds good. I hope you know how to play; I am a pretty good shot."

"Is that right? I guess we will just have to see, won't we?"

Marie and I proceed to play four games of pool and have around double the amount of drinks at the same time. Marie was good at pool. She beat me the first three games. I was able to win the last game. I didn't tell her yet, but I tend to get better the drunker I get. I went and grabbed some chips and salsa for some snacks. This is the most fun I have had in a long time. Meanwhile, when I came back with the snacks, there is Marie sitting on the side of the pool table with a devilish grin.

"What's that look you got going on? Looks like you have a devious plan." I said cautiously.

"You down to up the stakes for this next game? Let's have some fun."

"I am always down. What do you got in mind that you will lose to?"

"Confident, aren't ya? Even though I just beat you three to one. Well, this game we are going to have to drink every time the other makes a shot. As well as take off a piece of clothing. Strip and drink pool. Are you game or will you chicken out?"

"It's on. Little did you know I get better as I drink. Prepare to be drunk and naked."

"We'll see about that. You won last game, so you get to break."

It's funny because I normally don't have that type of confidence to say something like that to a girl. Liquid courage gives me just that, and I definitely relax more than I normally can. Marie racks up the balls and I get the cue ball placed, ready to break. I focus really hard and give the ball a good whack with all my might. A very loud crash and the balls break, flying in every which way of the table. A very good break that separates all the balls. Thirteen ball sinks into the corner. I look over at Marie with a big smile.

"Ok hot shot, this needs to last awhile, so each article of clothing counts. Not pairs." Marie says as she throws her drink back and downs it. Next, she removes one shoe, following with what she said about pairs. Makes sense, being there are fifteen balls on the table. I take my next shot and boom, there's another ball. I just glance at Marie and she shakes her head while taking her drink and removing her other shoe.

"I forgot to ask, for this game are we playing eight ball, or are we just trying to sink any ball?" I asked.

"Any ball, makes things more interesting." Marie responds.

"That's what I was hoping you would say."

I then go on to sink three more in a row. Marie has now removed both of her socks and removed her shirt. She now only has on a bra, miniskirt, and I am assuming underwear. I've already sunk five of the balls. I am not sure what would happen if I sunk all fifteen when she clearly doesn't have that much clothing on. I am getting distracted just thinking about it. I am looking at Marie, admiring her amazing figure. Fantasizing about what she would look like without all the clothes.

"Earth to Mark. Are you going to shoot, or are you forfeiting your turn?"

"Oh shit, sorry. I got distracted."

"I could see that." Marie answered while leaning forward and putting her hands on the table. She knows exactly what she's doing there, distracting me even more. It's hard to concentrate on the shot I am trying to take when Marie is standing there flaunting the top of her breasts. Is it getting hot in here? I thought to myself. Ok, here I go. Boom, I take the shot, but this time I miss.

"I saw what you did there Marie. That's dirty." I say, fumbling my words with excitement.

"I don't have the slightest idea of what you're talking about Mr. Mark." Marie said while having that devious smirk again.

Marie grabs her stick and sinks 2 balls back to back. Fuck, she is really good. I remove both shoes and take both drinks. That makes seven balls down total. She stalks the table, walking around looking for which ball she is going to prey on, then whack. Two more down, like it was nothing. Both socks get removed now. Two more drinks.

"At this rate, I am going to pass out, and fast." I say with a drunken slur.

Marie doesn't even pay attention and boom, one more down. My shirt is now thrown across the room. I think she was playing me on how good she really was. I think she let me win that last game, just to boost my confidence. Smiling, she looks up at me as she takes her next shot and once again, clean sink. Pants are now on the floor.

"Well, I'll be damned Mark. Looks like you seem to of lost almost all of your clothes. You were doing so well in the beginning. You have one thing left on and there's four more balls. I guess we will have to make up some stipulations when we get to that point, won't we?"

Marie takes her next shot. It feels as if it's moving in slow motion. The unthinkable happens. The ball bounces out of the pocket. Now it's my turn.

At this point, I know it is do or die, well do or get naked. I guess explains it better. I try to concentrate on my next shot; I am really drunk at this point. Boom, take my shot and right to the corner pocket. Smiling, I look up at her while she drops her skirt to the ground. She is wearing a lacey black thong. Focus Mark, don't get distracted again. There are three balls left. Next shot, side pocket with ease. I don't even look up and take the next shot, corner pocket. Without hesitation, I then sink the last ball.

"Well, well, well. Looks like I was right. Looks like you will be drunk and naked. I just so happen to win." I say with drunken pride.

"A deal is a deal, Mr. Mark."

Marie then unhinges her bra and takes it off, revealing her perfectly shaped breasts, and throws it at me. She then removes her thong, revealing that every part of her body is silky smooth. Wow, I am in awe. I can't help but stare at her. I am speechless at this point.

"Well, Mark, I have my clothes off, but there was one extra ball made. So what's the stipulation for that one?" Marie said, smiling confidently.

"Uh... uh... um... I don't know. How about you

have to go jump in the pool?"

Without hesitation, Marie runs opens the back door and dives into the pool. At this point I look down and realize I was more excited than I thought and risen to the occasion. I hear Marie calling for me to come join her and that the water felt amazing. Panicking, not wanting to run out there with a rock hard boner, I look around and grab the bottle of bourbon with one hand. Then, with the other hand, I grab the big bowl of chips and put the salsa inside the bowl. I now can walk outside and hold the bowl in front of me so I can hide my untimely erection. Running outside, go to the table by the sun beds. I set the bottle and bowls down. I glance down and with my pleasant surprise; I was no longer at full mast. Turning around, I run and jump into the pool.

"Cannon ball!"

I make a giant splash and just float for what feels like an eternity, when in reality it was only two seconds before I swam up to have my head above water. Wow, sometimes you forget how good it feels to swim while intoxicated. The sensations you get from the water gliding around your skin, as if you're floating, yet gently being caressed at the same time. I'm not sure if she did this on purpose, but Marie was swimming backwards, floating on top of the water, and swam right into me. Her head just missing my face, but the collision made the rest of her body fall down into the water. Her juicy ass just so happened to press against my nether regions, which caught me off guard. The feeling of her plump, but firm derriere falling against me; which also felt like it had an extra push to it sent an electric shock to my whole body. I couldn't even comprehend how good that brief touch had felt. She turned around and faced me. With a slur, Marie says, "Oh shit, I didn't even see you there."

"It's ok. I didn't mind the crash." I responded.

At this point, we are both towards the shallow end of the pool and we are standing. We are still very close, only what seems a few inches between us. I notice her breasts are bobbing up and down with the waves of the pool in which I can't help but look. Marie says, "Mark, are you staring at my tits?"

"Ah.... Shit, ok, you caught me. I couldn't help it; they were bobbing up and down with the pool. I'm sorry."

"Tsk, tsk Mark. You need to have better manors." Marie said sarcastically.

In what seemed to be slow motion, Marie was moving closer to me. She was bringing her face towards mine. I was watching her move; it didn't feel real. At that moment, her mouth reached mine, in which we embraced with what felt like the most magical kiss I had ever felt in my life. It felt as if we were spinning, rising out of the water. All the while happening in slow motion. My eyes couldn't even open, yet my hands are caressing her smooth skin. Running slowly from the top of her shoulders with my fingertips down to the lower back. I grab her ass with both of my hands, squeezing with excitement. I am in such bliss that I can't even believe what is happening. As we get more comfortable with each other's bodies, there was a flash of light. Then another. We freeze and both look over to the back door of my house and we see Braden with a big smile, taking pictures of us on his phone. Right at this moment, I realize that the feeling I had of floating and spinning wasn't actually a feeling. It was reality; I was floating above my pool while embraced with Marie. I shudder and let go of Marie while squirming and fall back into the water. After I emerge from under the water, I look over at Braden and yell at him, "You motherfucker! You better delete that shit."

Braden yells back, "Fuck no, time to expose you motherfuckers."

Braden puts his phone into his pant pocket and runs towards my gate. There is absolutely no way I can reach him before he gets out. At this point, I know we are fucked. I look back at Marie; she has this look on her face. Like she is in some sort of trance. She raises her hand out of the water, towards Braden. She's saying something that I can't quite understand and moves her hand fast in the direction of Braden. I look back at Braden and a vine from a tree flies towards him and grabs him by the arm. Then another grabs his other arm. Now both legs are bound as well. What the fuck.

chapter 7

Holy shit! I have no idea what I am seeing right now. Is this real life? I don't even know how to process what is happening. Were we really floating while kissing? How did those vines fly from the trees and grab a hold of Braden? I... I don't know what to do. Braden is bound. I am in the pool standing; unable to move. Marie is a few feet in front of me, walking to the stairs to get out of the pool. Oh my god, she did that. She made all these things happen. Who is she? Better question, what is she? Is she a sorcerer? A witch? Some sort of demon? What is she going to do to Braden? What is she going to do to me afterward? What do I do? Ok Mark, get a hold of yourself. This is really happening.

I look at Marie, blinking, wondering if this is real life. I know it is; I have come to the realization that I am not in a dream. That this is, in fact, actually happening. I start to scramble and rush to get out of the pool. I get to the edge and stop myself. This might be a stupid thing to do, but I am drunk, here goes nothing...

"Marie. What in the actual fuck is going on?" I said timidly.

"Mark, you are just going to have to trust me." Marie replied.

"Trust you? What are you going to do? More importantly, what are you?"

"I will explain everything after. First, I need to deal with the ass hat."

Deal with him? What does she mean by that? Is she going to kill him? Torture him? I think I am about to witness a murder. The strange thing is I don't feel threatened by her. She makes me comfortable, even though she might do something vicious right now. Is it because I am drunk? I think my buzz wore off by now. Is it because she's beautiful? It doesn't help that she is still completely naked.

Marie gets out of the pool and walks over to Braden. I hop out of the pool and follow shortly behind her. I keep my distance, but I want to know what is going on. Marie gets right in front of Braden. She doesn't say a word and reaches into his pant pocket and grabs his phone.

"There's more for you to grab in there." Braden says with a big smile. "I don't mind that you're into this bondage stuff. With a body like that, you can do whatever you want to me."

"Shut up, pig." Marie says angrily.

Marie takes his phone and holds it in her palm with her right hand her facing up. She focuses on the phone and it levitates. In mid-air, it basically implodes into dust. I am just standing by the table, watching in awe. I grab the bottle of bourbon and take a nice big swig. I am definitely going to need some more of this.

"Now, what am I going to do with you now that the evidence is gone?" Marie expresses. "Maybe I should have your skin peel itself from your body. Have it slowly rip off. Or should I summon some wolves to eat you alive? I think I am just going to erase your memory. Yea, that's exactly what I will do. You're lucky I am happy here and like Mark. The old me would have killed you and fed your organs to the animals in the forest."

I could see the shock on Braden's face. He looks terrified. I am kind of happy about that if I am being honest with myself. She said that she's going to make him forget what he's seen here. How is she going to do that? I might be even more confused than before. I am just going to keep drinking this bourbon. Is she going to make me forget everything too? I am so frazzled. I don't even know what to think. Part of me is terrified. The other part of me is intrigued. Excited even. Really drunk again, that's for sure.

Marie looks up at me and winks with a smile.

She snaps her fingers and this table with a black candle, a bowl, and some sort of book appeared in front of her. I see her put some things into the bowl. Looks like herbs. She poured what appears to be some sort of oil into the bowl. I think she is chanting something while doing all of this as well. Marie picked up the bowl and held it under Braden's left hand. She grabbed at the table, which appeared to be empty, but pulled a dagger out of thin air. She makes a minor cut in Braden's hand. He appears to be in some sort of trance; he doesn't make a noise. Even in a trance, it appears he's still his perverted self and staring at her tits, of course. His blood is dripping into the bowl. Marie sets the bowl back on the table along with the dagger that disappears into the table again.

Marie raises her arms up, straightened from her side and level with her shoulders. The candle ignites with a flame that is somehow three feet high. She picks up the black candle and tilts it sideways above the bowl to let some of the wax spill into it. She sets the candle back down and puts her hands over the bowl. The bowl now bursts into flames. The flames are changing color from the normal orange to blue, then to green, last to black, and then self-extinguishes. She now puts her fingers into the substance inside the bowl and rubs it across Braden's head. Moving from the center of his forehead to both sides of his head, using both hands synchronically.

Braden's face is wincing in agony. He looks like he's trying to belt out a scream. Nothing is coming out of his mouth though. After about five seconds, his head just drops forward. It appears he has passed out. Hopefully, that's all he did. Those five seconds felt like ten minutes to me. I still am in shock. I am witnessing this in real life. Am I dreaming? I pinch myself. Nope, still real life. Doesn't matter how many times I keep checking. Marie raises her arms in swift motions, chanting. Then she stops and freezes, standing in an upright position. The candle flame goes out. She claps her hands in front of her while dropping her head down and Braden disappeared. The table is now gone as well. Marie lifts her head up and looks over at me. Now she is walking towards me. What am I in for?

chapter 8

She looks like she's moving in slow motion. What am I going to do? I am in shock after what I have just seen. I have no idea if something bad is going to happen to me. Is she going to kill me? What happened to Braden? What is she? I have so many questions. I don't know what to think at this point. Should I run? I don't think running will get me anywhere, anyway. Marie is in front of me. She's saying something, but I can't make out any of the words. Am I having a panic attack?

Marie snaps her fingers next to my face. I wake up from what appears to be some sort of trance. I shake my head, realizing what is going on. Only thinking that my ride on this planet has ended. Nice knowing you world. Wish I could've done more.

Marie calmly says, "Mark, I know what you must be thinking. You are wondering how I did all that. I am also sure you have many more questions. So go right ahead and ask."

"Ok... WHAT THE FUCK..."

"Calm down Mark, no need to get loud."

"BUT...BUT...HOW DID YOU... AND THEN... DISAPPEARED... FLYING... I... I... WHAT THE FUCK MARIE?"

"Mark, you need to sit down. Do you want another drink?"

I was pacing around like a cat that had catnip and now has the zoomies. Marie was sitting at the patio table and patting the chair in front of her. She was smiling at me and nodding as if to show me it will be ok. I need to focus on one thing at a time, just like she said. Ok, take some nice deep breaths. If Marie was planning on hurting me, I am pretty sure something would've happened by now. Let's figure this out. I always knew there was something special about her. Drink. I need another drink, definitely. I just point at the bottle and nod. I look back at Marie, wow she's so stunning. Her beauty kind of relaxes me and makes me feel comfortable. I guess it helps that she is still naked as well. That's a plus. I walk over to the chair and sit down. I look at my cup, which is empty. Marie looks at the cup as well, then she snaps her fingers and the cup is full. Taken aback by this, I jump a little. I guess this is going to be my real life now. This shit just got real. I take a sip. That is the best damn drink I've ever had. Here goes nothing. Time to get some goddamn answers.

"Ma... Ma... Marie, what the fuck did I just witness?"

"Mark, I am a witch. What you witnessed were my powers."

"What happened to Braden?"

"I erased his memory and now he is sleeping

in his bed comfortably. He won't remember anything."

"Ok. Do you plan on hurting me, or making me forget my memory? Or anyone in town, for that matter?"

"No Mark, I would never hurt you. I really like you. I don't want you to forget this. You know now, this makes me thrilled. Also, I would not hurt anyone in town."

"Ok. Why are you in Forestdale? Do you have some sort of plan to take over the city or something?"

"Ha, ha, ha. No Mark. I wasn't planning on sticking around. I was going to keep moving city to city. But then I met you. So I decided to maybe stick around for a while."

"Ok, where are you from? Why were you jumping from town to town?"

"I am not really from anywhere. My old coven was nomadic, so there was no actual hometown. I am also on the run because of my old coven. I ran away from them. They wanted me to do unspeakable things. They wanted me to sacrifice animals and people, yes people. I was supposed to slaughter my grandmother at the dinner table. She was already dying. She actually wanted to die. I couldn't do it. So I ran until I finally got away from them."

"I need some more alcohol."

At that point, Marie and I sat at the table on my back patio, drinking until five in the morning. We were both incredibly wasted. The sun was about to rise, so we figured it was time to go to bed. Marie said she was ok to drive home, but I told her not a chance in hell. Even if she would only ride her broom. She thought that was funny. As we stumble inside, I tell her she can sleep in my bed and I will sleep in the guest room. I grab her by the arm and walk her upstairs. Both of us were laughing and bouncing off the walls as we attempted to ascend the narrow staircase. I get to the top and open up my room door. We both walk in and I throw back the black silk sheets with my dark Victorian comforter that is embroidered with golden designs and flowers. I usher her into the bed. She turned to me and said, "You don't have to sleep in the guest room. This is your bed. You sleep in it too, at least." As drunk as I was, I did not protest it. My bed was the best in the house, anyway. I just dove onto the bed and crawled my way up to the middle.

"Marie, I think you being a witch is bad fucking ass!"

"Thanks, Mark. I was really worried that you would fear me and never talk to me again."

"Are you kidding? It scared me shitless when I saw you using your powers."

"Why didn't you run? Or scream, or whatever."

"I don't know. Part of me was just frozen in shock. The other part of me thought it was incredible. Besides, you're incredibly hot, and naked, so I couldn't take my eyes off of you."

"So if I had clothes on, would you have run away then?"

"No, you're still hot with clothes on."

At that moment, Marie turned towards me and moved her head close to mine. I took the hint, and I moved forward towards her. Our faces met, and we shared a very drunken yet very passionate kiss. Marie's hands running through my hair, caressing my head as our lips are locked and our tongues are gliding along each other as if they already knew how to dance together. My hands have now grown a mind of their own and are exploring Marie's body. She is soft, and so silky smooth. She feels like what the embodiment of a goddess would feel like. Marie's hands have now started to explore my body. I have never been so turned on. I have now started to explore her body with my mouth. I am kissing her, starting from her forehead and moving my way down to her neck.

I kiss and lick the side of her neck. I blow on it lightly just to give her a little tingle. I then kiss it again and give it a little bite, not hard, but just to get a little reaction. I continue to move down her body and kiss her amazing breasts. I suck on each nipple; they stay hard. I move down more to her belly. I slowly slide to the left side, where I grab her hand and pull it to my face. I kiss and bite her wrist and hand. I do the same to the other hand and wrist as well. I come back to the center of her stomach, just below her navel. I move my head down quickly to her thighs. She laughs and calls me a tease.

I move my head slowly up her left thigh, kissing and licking. Then do the same to the right leg. Her skin tastes sweet. It's almost as if she bathes in honey. I am purposely taking my time to tease her. She can't take it anymore and grabs my head and pulls it to where she wants it. Kissing, licking, teasing and bringing my fingers in. One hand teasing the clitoris, the other inserting, while using my tongue as well. Marie is moaning and squirming until she pulls my head up and she says it's her turn.

She kisses my neck, but she doesn't mess around. She moves her head quickly down the front of my body, kissing and licking. She gets to my abs where she stops for a second and says damn. I guess the hard work at the gym has been paying off. She reaches down and grabs my dick. At this point, it is rock solid. She strokes my shaft and moves her head down. She does things that feel so amazing. Nothing I have ever felt before. The way she can move her tongue around and take the entirety had me paralyzed in absolute bliss. She moves off. She is now moving up on top of me. She now gets on top of my lap, where she inserts me into her.

The slow momentum of her going up and down with such passion. I can't take it anymore; I want to ravish her. I sit up and put my right arm around her back and post up on my left arm. I lift my body and swing her down on to her back. I kiss her and thrust my body into hers. I move faster and faster, harder and harder. I post my arms up and increase the momentum. I spin her over onto her hands and knees while kneeling up and grabbing her by her amazing ass. I smack her ass with one hand and reach under to squeeze her tits with the other. She then pushes me back to my back while facing away from me in reverse cowgirl. I can tell at this point she is getting close to climax, so am I. Looking around, I realize we are now floating in the middle of the room. We are hovering over my bed and I laugh to myself, thinking I just became the witch's broom. Our orgasm came at the same time, which felt like an explosion of pleasure that I have never experienced before. I can attest that truly, witches do it better.

The sound of the shower running woke me up. I lift my head up and look around to realize that Marie isn't in the bed, meaning she is hopefully the one inside the shower. Grumbling, I say, "ow, my fucking head is killing me." I hear Marie say it's ok, I got you. Marie comes out of the bathroom with a little black robe on. "Where did you get a robe?" I asked.

"Witch, remember? All I had to do was snap my fingers. Now let me brew something up for you real quick and we will get rid of that hangover."

"Ok Marie, sounds great."

Marie then snaps her fingers again, and a small black cauldron appears in front of her. Along with what looked like a book and a bag. The book is floating in front of her and she is grabbing ingredients out of the bag. She throws all the ingredients inside and stirs. A green smoke puffs out, and she pulls out a glass from the bag. She pours some of the mystery liquid into the glass and hands it to me. She says drink up buttercup. I look at it and say I don't even want to know what's in it. Bottoms up, I drink it all real fast. Surprisingly, it didn't taste bad at all. In fact, it tasted like fruit punch oddly enough. Around five seconds later, all of my hangover symptoms went away. I felt better than I normally do. I look at Marie and say, "I could get used to this hangover cure. You are one incredible woman, Marie."

chapter 9

At this point, we are basically inseparable. I have never felt so alive than when I am with Marie. She picks me up and we stroll around town in her Jeep. We take Ginger out for walks at night time. The endless amounts of dirty looks and ignorant gestures we get amongst the town are one of the things I look forward to the most. I love seeing everyone getting their panties in a bunch over us having the time of our lives. Braden has no recollection of what happened the night he came over. Now he basically tries to be our friend and hang out with us as much as he can. He gets annoying, though. He shows up unannounced at my house. Surprisingly though, now we all have a lot of fun together. Marie just doesn't use any magic when he's around. Well, at least none that he will see or notice. Marie's cooking, on the other hand, should be considered magic because it is that good. She doesn't use any magic to make the food either, quite amazing.

Just when I thought everything seems like it was too good to be true, I was right. I was in town by myself going to the store to pick up some food to make when I saw a strange man I have never seen before. I was treading carefully, trying to watch him and see what he was doing without him noticing me. He was talking to some of the other townies in the store. It looked like he was asking them questions, but they just kind of shrugged. Then they looked over at me and pointed. Fuck, what is this about? The man gives his thanks and then makes his way over to me.

The man walks up and reaches his hand out

to me to shake my hand. I comply and reciprocate; I make sure I give a nice, firm handshake. He gives a half smile and says, "Hi, my name is Silas. I am from out of town. I am looking for a friend of mine and those kind people over there said that you could help me out."

"Is that right? Is that what they told you? Not sure how much help I can be, but I will do the best I can."

"Thank you, and your name is?"

"My name is Mark. Now, who is it you are looking for, Silas?"

"I am looking for a blonde girl named Marie. She's real pretty."

"Marie, yea, I know a Marie with blonde hair that is really pretty. You said she's an old friend of yours? She's not your girlfriend, is she?"

"No, no, no. She is more like a sister, I guess you could say. That's good that you know her. Where can I find her? I need to meet up with her."

"I don't know where she is staying, actually.

If I see her again, I will let her know you are in town and looking for her. Is there a place I can tell her where she can find you?"

"Yes, I am staying at the Robertson's motel in town. Room 31, I will be waiting."

"Alright Silas, I will let her know if I see her."

I knew there was something wrong here. Call it intuition, but I got a very disturbing vibe from this guy. Obviously, he was one of the people from her old coven. I need to figure out a way to see Marie without Silas getting any hints that I have seen her. I need to warn her he has come to our town. Does this mean that there are more here as well? This can't be good. Marie said they wanted to do some really terrible things. Let's hope they don't plan on carrying out those things in our town.

I am going to just go home and hope that Marie senses I want her to meet me there. I pull up to my home, no jeep. Shit, I need to figure out a way to contact her. I walk inside and sit down in the living room on the couch. Let me try this meditation thing she is always talking about.

Maybe if I focus on her and that I have a message for her, she will receive it. How did she say to do it again? Oh yea, get comfortable, sit upright, she said. I didn't have to cross my legs, right? That's right, she said whatever is comfortable. Close your eyes, go blank, think of nothing, and just focus on my breath. Breathe in, breathe out. In, out, in, out. Ok, I am feeling relaxed. Focus now, Marie, if you can hear me, or feel me, or whatever the fuck that would be. Please come to my house. I have something really important to tell you. Marie, I repe—.

"Mark, is everything ok? I could sense you were distraught."

"Wow, that actually worked?"

"Yes, I could feel you calling for me, like a need for me."

"I did your meditating thing and was calling out for you. Wow, I didn't expect it to work that easily."

"Ok, well, what's the problem? What did you need me to be here so fast for?"

"I met someone real interesting in the store

today. Someone that was looking for you. His name was Silas."

"Fuck. Did you just say Silas was in town?"

"Yes, he was at the store asking people if they know who you were. They pointed over to me so I didn't have any choice but to talk to him."

"Oh shit, what did you say? What did he say?"

"He asked if I knew you, which I said I did. Then he asked if I knew where you were or how to get ahold of you."

"Mother fuck. What did you say?"

"I take it this guy is not a good guy? I said I didn't know how to get ahold of you. But if I saw you, I would let you know he was in town. He is staying at the Robertson's motel, room 31. Look, it's not any of my business, but if there's something wrong, please let me know."

"Mark, he is the High fucking Priest of the coven! He is a very dangerous person. Now you are in his crosshairs. He knows you know me. This could be very dangerous."

"Ok, well shit. What do we do?"

"This was a mistake. I should've kept

running. I need to go see him. He will do some fucked up shit if I don't. He knows that if I found out he was here, I would have two choices. One, run and he would decimate the whole town to spite me. Two, face the music and go see him."

"What is he going to do if you go see him? Can't you just ask him to leave you alone? That you are done with them?"

"HA, yea right. Most likely, he will cast some sort of binding spell on me and drag me back to the coven. Or threaten to kill everyone until I comply with him and do as I am told. I am so sorry, Mark, that I got you mixed up in this."

"No fucking way. I am not letting you go anywhere. You and I have something. I am not willing to give this up. I don't care if he is the god damned messiah. I won't let anyone take you away from me."

"No offense Mark, but what are you going to do? He is really powerful."

"I don't know yet. I have guns. I know guns will hurt him... Right?"

"Yes, weapons can hurt us. It's just a matter of

if someone can actually use them on us."

"Ok, well, we can work with this. Let's make a plan. Let's figure out what we can do. Maybe for now. Let's pretend I haven't seen you yet and wait to see what he does."

"Ok, yea. Let's do that. Let's just pretend I haven't met up with you recently. I won't go into town. I'll just come here or be in my spot in the woods. I won't use my jeep either. I will just teleport myself back and forth. How did he know I was here?"

"One day at a time. One thing at a time. That's all we can do, I guess. For now, let's make some steaks, and do you have any more of that bourbon? "

"Yea, steaks and bourbon. I do, let me grab it. (snap) Here you go."

"It is going to take me a while to get used to that."

"Most people run scared when they even see any of our powers. So I know there is something special when you aren't even scared in the slightest."

"Honestly, it's sexy."

We continued to flirt, and drink, and eat. This continued on for a few hours until we found ourselves making our way to the bedroom. Time to blow off some stress. Even though we were having a good time right now, it was hard to keep Silas out of my head. If Marie was scared of him, he must be powerful. Pretty soon he will realize that I tipped her off, too. We really need to make some sort of plan. I know I am going to run into him again. I am sure it will be sooner than later.

chapter 10

Two weeks pass, and nothing has happened. I haven't even seen Silas in town. I don't know if I should be worried or scared shitless. Marie seems to think that Silas is holding out and just waiting to strike at the perfect moment. The bad part about that, she knows him best. I guess until then, we will just have to wait and see what happens.

It would appear that I have spoken too soon. I had gone into town to buy essentials. Get the usual food items to make a nice dinner, drinks, the usuals. As I walked into the store, I noticed that there was something different, off. The people who worked at the store were the only ones who were present. There seemed to be even fewer workers than normal too. There's a weird tension in the air as well.

I grabbed all my produce, watermelons, mangos, strawberries, all the sweet tasting yummy fruits that would also be good mixers or chasers. Now I am making my way back to the meat counter where I suspect I will see Braden. Things have been better with him since he basically got his brain reprogrammed by Marie. Again, such a weird thing to say, but that is my normal life now. As I turn the corner or the isle, I see him standing next to the meat counter. It is Silas. He appears to be waiting for someone, and I am pretty sure that someone is me.

I walk up and say, "Hey buddy, how's it going? If I remember correctly, Silas, right?"

"Cut the shit." Silas bellows. "I know you have seen her, yet she has not come to see me. I also know you know what she is. I can smell her magic on you."

"Whoa, whoa, whoa, did you just say magic?"

"Oh Marky Mark, you really shouldn't play stupid with me. I know exactly what you are up to. Hiding her from me will not work. I am going to have to be a little irrational to get my point across."

"What? What do you mean?"

"I will show you what that means."

Silas stepped back and started to move his hands around in elegant formations. Then he chants.

One of the people who worked at the store walked around the corner. An older woman with shoulder length red hair. She made her way to Silas and asked, "Hi, is there anything I can hel—"

Silas threw his arms out to the side, and the woman froze, replicating the same stance that Silas was posing. I could see in her eyes she was aware what was happening. The only thing was, she could not respond. She could not make a sound; she could not control her body. I look at Silas, shocked. I could not say a word. I was dumbfounded on the events that were taking place in front of my eyes. He continues to chant and use his hand movements while she stays in place as if she was crucified to the air. Silas then threw his right hand in front of him as if he was holding a large bowl in front of his face. He swung his hand clockwise in a circular formation and the woman's head now faced behind her. The only odd thing about it was that her body did not drop at this point.

Her body was convulsing, yet barely moving as if being held by a powerful force that was not allowing it to move. Silas now moved his hands up, but spreading them wider at this point. He turned his hands upside down. The woman's floating corpse was now flipped inverse as well. Silas threw one hand sideways fast and the woman's neck split on one side from the top of her head, now basically touching her elbow from sliding over her shoulder. The blood is now pouring out of her neck. Silas is now using his hand as if he is writing something in the air. Astonished, I am only watching him. He looks at me and winks. Poof, thin air. He is gone. The body drops to the floor. As I look to the ground, the blood spells out, "Marie, you have two days. There will be two more bodies for every day I have to wait."

As disturbing as it was, the writing was quite magnificent. You don't see very well written words like that anymore. After being mesmerized by the writing technique, I realized what the actual words said. In a panic, I took a picture so I can show Marie. What the fuck will I do to explain this though? Someone is bound to see this crime scene and look at me like I am a crazy person. Then, suddenly, poof, the body was gone. The blood is gone. Not a trace that any of that even happened. What are they going to think when they realize the worker is gone? Will they see this on the cameras?

"Oh shit, oh fuck. Shit, fuck. SHIT! FUCK!"

I am starting to panic. What do I do? WHAT THE FUCK DO I DO?

Ok, I need to tell Marie what is going on, and fast. I literally ran out of the store. I bought nothing. I left my cart where it was and just left.

chapter **11**

Day one. Sitting in my backyard trying to figure out what on earth can we do to possibly get past what just happened. I feel like I have just been tossed around in a tornado. My emotions are everywhere. I am freaking out. I cannot sit down. Pacing back and forth, drinking, not eating much besides a couple of bites of watermelon and steak. Ginger is following me back and forth, waiting for me to drop pieces of steak. I don't actually drop any, but while holding it, my hand is to my side, and she snags it from me. I am too distracted to pay attention that she is taking the steak from my hand.

"Marie, what the fuck are we going to do? He killed that woman so fast and with no remorse."

"Mark, this is what I was trying to tell you before. I can't run from him if he knows I know he is here. He will just kill everyone in town to make a statement. I should just face the facts and go back to the coven."

"Why is this so important to him? Why do they care if you go back or don't? I don't understand any of this. Well, no shit, what am I thinking? Of course I don't understand any of this. I barely just found out about magic, and witches, and all this shit. HA HA, what the fuck has my life turned into?"

"I am sooo sorry Mark. I never should've burdened you with getting into your life." Marie said sarcastically.

"Shit, I am sorry Marie. I didn't mean it that way. But you have to understand that my world not only just turned upside down, but it was also turned inside out at the same time. So many things that I never knew before have just changed and transformed my whole life, forever. I am thrilled that it was with you and that I know you."

"I know. This is just stressful. You should just let me go. Let me fix this and disappear. Everyone and everything will be safe. Simple."

"Sure, that would be easy. It would fix everything and all would be well. Except you and me. We have something special. I refuse to let that go. You don't deserve to get trapped in that terrible coven that will force you to do things you don't want to do. We need to figure out a way to fight. We need to kill Silas. If we do that, will that keep them from coming after you?"

"I guess it could work. Cut the head off the snake and you won't have to worry about the rest of it."

"Ok, well, I guess we are on the same page. We need to make a plan. We need more than just a plan. We need to be prepared for any outcome. You said weapons can hurt him, so that's a start.

Guns, I have a lot of guns. They would need to be used when he least expected any of that to happen. Got any ideas?"

"I think we should act like I am going with him. At the last minute, before the time is up. I will go to his motel and tell him I am going to come with him. You can shoot him the moment he gets into the door frame."

"I have a long-range rifle. I can shoot it from across the parking lot. Good thing I have all that hunting experience. He won't even see it coming. We should have a Plan B as well. Maybe you can carry a gun with you in case I miss or somehow, he evades it. When he gets distracted with me, you could shoot him from behind."

"That could work. Yes. Maybe we should have a plan C as well. Like, let's loop in Braden. Get him to be on the other side of the parking lot. Or in a different spot, so he could be an element of surprise with another rifle."

"Yes, that will have to do. We will have to bring him in. Have another ally. We need to be really careful. Fuck Marie, this is some scary shit.

He should be alone, right? I just thought about that. If he is the leader of the coven, why would he not bring anyone with him?"

"He has a big ego. There's a good chance he is by himself. He likes to prove he's the head honcho. But I guess there is a chance someone is with him. We only have one chance at this though, so we will just have to risk it. Worst-case scenario, someone is with him and I will just have to go with them. End of story."

"Ok, well, I guess it's time to call Braden over. Loop him into the plan. Hope that he is actually wanting to join in on this. You will have to show him magic too. Hope he doesn't flip out. Fuck, there is so much that he is going to need to digest from this. I can't even relax for one second."

"I know what will make you relax."

At that moment, Marie got up from her chair. She walked over to me and grabbed me by the arm. She pulled me back to her chair, where she sat back down. She then undid my belt, open the button and unzip my pants. She then pulls down my pants and boxer briefs where she grabbed on to my cock. Slowly stroking it until she puts her warm mouth on it and continues to move her head while doing those magical things she does with her tongue. This is definitely making me relax. I need to ask if there is some sort of magical element she uses to this, because I have never felt a blowjob feel this amazing. For the next however many minutes of bliss, I could forget about the entire problem situation.

Fully relaxed, I sit down in complete contempt. Everything feels better at this point. I don't feel so stressed out. My mind is clear and I am ready to focus on planning. This woman is magical in every aspect. If that is sex magic, count me in.

"All better Mark?" Marie says with a sexy smirk.

"I can't even explain how much of the world's problems have just disappeared for me."

"Glad I could help."

"Alright, I guess it's time to call Braden over. Let's hope he will be game."

I text Braden and tell him I need him to come over now. I put it is very important, life or death important. He responds with omw. Meaning he is on his way. Here we go, time to blow his mind with what the world is actually capable of. Well, I guess for the second time.

Braden arrived about fifteen minutes later. He came rushing through the front door. He ran to the backyard and said, "Mark, what's the big fucking emergency?"

"Braden, you are going to want to take a seat for what I am about to tell you."

"Ok, this better be something crazy, otherwise I am going to kick you in the dick for making such a big deal."

Braden took a seat. Although he would never admit it, he was definitely nervous. Marie came outside bringing three cups and her special bourbon. Hopefully, the bourbon will also work as a calming agent for Braden.

"Braden, I am just going to come out with it bluntly. Marie is a witch. People from her coven have come here and are threatening to kill everyone in town."

"Seriously Mark? What the fuck? You made it sound like an emergency for a stupid prank like this?"

"Braden, it's not a joke. Seriously, watch. Marie do something magical to show him."

Marie stood up and put her right hand out in front of her. Flames rose from her palm, in which seemed like they were five feet high. Braden had a puzzled look on his face. He also didn't look very convinced. Marie also noticed this, that's when she walked out of the patio to the grass. She took off her clothes and was standing there in her bra and thong. She raised her arms and chanted. Rain poured on her. She jumped into the pool and then she floated up and out of the pool. Marie then snapped her fingers, and the rain stopped. She grabbed her clothes, walked back to where we were and grabbed a towel. Marie handed me the towel to hold up for her in which she then took off the rest of what she was wearing. I wrapped her up with the towel and she sat down, grabbed a cup and looked at Braden as she drank.

"Mark. What the fuck did I just witness? She just made it rain. She flew out of the pool. That had a familiar feeling too. Holy shit. What in the actual fuck? But... How... What the... This, this can't be good. Mark, what have you gotten into? I... I don't know how to handle this."

"Braden, I know this is shocking and crazy and confusing all at the same time. I really need you to focus. This is not something we can fuck around with. There is a very dangerous person in our town who is going to kill everyone. I need your help to kill him before he can destroy our town. Can I rely on you?"

"WHAT? First you show me magic, now you are telling me you want me to help you murder someone? What the fuck? Who are you?"

"Braden, take a fucking drink. Relax, I know this is insane. I need you, man. I need you more than ever so that we can save our town. Please, tell me you are with us?"

Before there was any more confusion and mental turmoil. Marie drinks the entirety of her cup, stands up and drops the towel. Completely naked, she walks and jumps in the pool and swims. I think she partially just giving us some time to talk alone, but also to distract with her beautiful naked body. There's a certain level of magic in seeing that sight that will make anyone want to be compliant.

"First off Mark, holy shit, she is hot! I think I understand how you got sucked into this now."

"You have no idea. She definitely sucked me into this and not just with her looks."

"Wow, ok. Second, are you serious about what you said? Is there really someone here that is going to kill everyone if we don't kill them first?"

"Yes. It's that strange guy Silas that came to town a couple weeks ago. I am sure you have met him."

"Fuck, yea. He comes into the store all the time. Come to think about it, he just walks around talking to everyone. I don't think I have ever seen him buy anything."

"Well, are you ready to become a hero of our

town? They will never even know what we have done for them. But you will at least know you saved our entire town."

"Shit, I guess I don't have a choice. This is fucking crazy. I felt like I already knew she was a witch for some reason. Oh well, I guess at this point that doesn't really matter, anyway. Give me the rundown. What is the plan?"

I wave to Marie to come back and join the conversation. She gets out of the pool and walks back over to us and sits down. This time, she doesn't even cover herself up. I realize that her nude body gives off a certain level of comfortability. I am sure her bourbon is also helping settle the situation. We tell Braden all the details of the plan. We continue to drink and get looser as the night goes on. I cook up some steaks for us all. It is insane to think this is the reality of our lives at this point. I never thought I could trust Braden with this, but he is there for me when it counts, I guess. It only took a little memory loss to make us such good friends again. In two days, one of us will hopefully commit a murder. Another thing I never thought I would say. For the rest of tonight, I am going to enjoy drinking, eating, good conversation full of laughter, and watching a beautiful woman, my beautiful woman, dance and have a blast with us completely naked. In other circumstances, this would be one of my favorite nights ever.

chapter 12

Day two. Marie, Braden and I woke up around ten am. We are not exactly sober waking up, but we also don't have a hangover because of Marie's magical bourbon. I get up and make my way to the kitchen. I yell out to everyone, "Rise and shine. How does a bacon breakfast burrito sound?"

Braden just sits up on the couch and looks at me. He makes some sort of grumbling noise but nods his head yes. Marie walks out of my room wearing nothing but little black lacey underwear.

Marie is very comfortable not wearing much, if anything at all. I am not complaining. Marie smiles big and gives me a kiss.

"Good morning, Mark. I would love a breakfast burrito."

"Good morning, beautiful. Coming right up hot stuff. "

Braden looks at Marie and says, "Not sure if you are aware, but you are not wearing a shirt. Or much of anything at all."

"What Braden? You've never seen tits before? I don't really care about being naked or who sees me."

"Um, Mark, are you going to tell your woman to put some clothes on?" Said Braden.

"She's her own person. If she wants to walk around naked in my house, in my backyard, hell in the fucking forest. I don't own her. She can do whatever she wants, right? Besides, I am not complaining. I enjoy the view." Mark says with a big smile, looking at Marie.

"Fair enough. I am not complaining either." Braden responds.

"Ok, we really need to go over this plan time and time again. We cannot mess this up. We will only have one chance to do this. The worst part is we can't go scope it out in person. We will have to review it on Google Earth or something to try to get the lay of the land the best we can."

I know this is extremely dangerous, but there is a certain level of excitement to it. If there were different circumstances, I know this would be a lot of fun. I pulled up a view of the parking lot at the Robertson's motel and pinpoint where the hit should take place. We review repeatedly until it feels as if we exhausted every single thing that could happen. This will all take place tomorrow, so this whole day is going to feel nerve wrecking. Trying to keep a level head as well, so we aren't drinking. We don't want to try to assassinate an all-powerful witch with a hangover.

"Marie, what are some things that we should know about Silas? Like, is there anything that he is great at, or specializes in that we should be aware of?" I asked.

"Yea, he is good at all aspects of magic.

However, he specializes in controlling fire. He can do all sorts of things with fire. Or he can control someone's body." Marie answered.

"I know that one. What I saw him do to that poor lady in the store was insane. The way her head basically ripped off and her body turned into a big pen was disturbing."

"That is some real scary shit, guys. Maybe let's not talk about all the ways he can kill us before we go and try to assassinate him. K?" Braden said timidly.

I decided I was going to take out the guns that we will all be using so I can clean them and have them at peak performance for tomorrow. I grab my.338 Lapua Magnum; I want to make sure I won't miss. I grab the DDM4 for Braden to use. Another beautiful killing machine, just in case. Then our side arms Sig, Glock, and HK we will have for a backup.

I can't help but keep feeling like there is something we are missing. I don't know what, so I say nothing about it. It is really bothering me though. Marie walks up to me and asks, "What's bothering you?"

"How do you do that? I was just feeling like there is something we were missing. Like, there is a piece of the puzzle that is missing."

"I feel that way too. We have a good plan though. Maybe it is just our nerves playing games with us?"

"I hope so, I know we have a good plan. I just hope Silas doesn't have a good counter plan as well."

"Knowing Silas, I am sure he has some sort of contingency plan. I don't think he would expect all this firepower though. So hopefully we have enough element of surprise to take him down."

"Well, I guess there is only one way to find out."

We all decide to go to bed early tonight, except I don't think any of us will actually get much sleep at all. The plan is for Marie to go to the motel at noon. I am really hoping this plan works out smoothly, but something is telling me that there will be something we don't think about. It is very unnerving.

chapter *13*

am scared shitless. Today is the day we are going to assassinate, or at least attempt to assassinate, a very powerful being. A high priest in a powerful witch coven. Something I never thought I would ever say out loud or in my thoughts. This has become all too real.

06:30AM, everyone is awake. We all barely slept. I laid in bed with Marie till around

02:00AM, which was the last time I checked the clock. I could hear Braden fidgeting around, moving on the couch all night as well. It was a very uncomfortable feeling. I went to the kitchen and made some coffee. I asked who wanted some, but they both already had cups in hand when I turned around. Caffeine, we all needed lots of caffeine. I asked if anyone was hungry, in which we all agreed we did not want to eat at that time. We must eat at ten at least. That way, we had some food in us for fuel.

07:30AM, time for us all to take a shower and start getting ready for the day. There is a guest shower in the bathroom near the back docr I told Braden he could use. Marie and I will shower together in the master bathroom. I walk into the bathroom and turn on the water. I have one of the updated showers that has the overhead rain with steam and other directional shower heads. I open the glass door and Marie walks in; I take off my clothes and throw them off to the laundry basket in the corner and follow into the shower, shutting the door behind me.

I walk up to Marie, who is closing her eyes standing under the rainfall. We have the steam turned up pretty high, so the vision inside the shower is blurred a bit. I stand behind her and run my hands up and down her back. I massage her shoulders, squeeze her arms, and run my hands through her hair while rubbing her head. She leans her head back, with what looks like she could finally start relaxing.

Marie says, "That feels so good. Please, squeeze my whole body."

"I can definitely do that." I respond.

I continue to rub her head for around ten seconds. I then move my hands down to her neck. Then squeeze her shoulders. I massage her upper back and in-between her shoulder blades. I move down and massage her mid and lower back. I continue my way down and squeeze her ass; I massage it as well. I am now on the back of her legs, massaging her hamstrings. Now, I am kneeling on the ground of the shower as I continue down to her quads.

I turn her around and move her backwards

so she can sit on the built in tile bench seat against the wall. I am definitely happy I had that added for comfort. I pick up her right foot and squeeze and massage her foot and ankle. I massage my way all the way to the top of her right thigh. I set down her leg and do the same thing on the other leg. I now grab her right arm and squeeze and massage all the way down to her hand. I replicate the same thing to the other arm. Now I gently rub her face. I move my way down to the top of her chest, right in the muscle area of her pectorals. I drop my hands down and sneak a nice grab of her beautiful breasts.

I kneel back down and pick up her right leg again. I am now kissing my way up her leg. I start from the ankle and move all the way up to her inner thigh, but stop right before getting to the center. I grab her left leg now and replicate kissing my way up to the top of her inner thigh. Right before going to the center, I move my head right above and kiss her there. I push her legs open more, turn my head to the left and lick her thigh from bottom to top, still stopping right before. I turn my head to the right and do the same to her left leg. Only this time, when I get to the top, I kiss her where she wanted it the most. I continue to kiss, and now I am starting to use my tongue and lick her up and down. She quivers and moans as I lightly glide my hands up her thighs. I bring my right hand to her entrance, where I insert two fingers. Her body tenses and is shifting. I use my left thumb to play with her clit while I lick right below while also putting my two fingers from my right hand in and out of her simultaneously. I guess this is a benefit from being ambidextrous.

After continuing this for five minutes or so, Marie grabs my head and pulls me up.

"Ok Mark, I want you to fuck me now. Fuck me hard."

"You're the boss, baby."

I stand up and pull Marie up off of the seat. I grab her by the waist and twist her around and push her forward so she is bending over. I bend my knees to get a little lower and guide my cock into her entrance. I start off slowly, but escalate the tempo. Marie moans louder and louder. I am certain Braden can hear us; we zero fucks about it. I continue to thrust, over and over, for what seems like time has frozen and we are just on planet pleasure. I pull her up and press her against the glass door. Just as we reach our climax together, I wrap my arms around her and hold her tight. She turns her head toward me and kisses me with her rapid breath. She turns around and faces me. We look into each other's eyes, and without hesitation, we both say, "I love you."

I turn off the shower and grab our towels, still standing in the shower drying off. I cannot take my eyes off of her. I have to make sure our plan works out. I don't know why, but I cannot live without her. I am certain of that. Marie wraps her towel around her body as I wrap it around my waist. We both walk out of the shower and into the room where Braden was sitting on the bed. He looks up at us and slowly claps.

"Wow guys, maybe save some energy for our mission, huh? By the way, I had a clear view of the shower. Too bad it was too steamy for me to watch entirely. The part against the shower door though, that was an awesome touch." Braden said while holding his right hand up in an ok symbol.

"Wow Braden, that's creepy that you were watching us. Hope you enjoyed the show as much as I did. I doubt it though." Marie said with a smirk.

"Ok guys, get dressed. We need to load up the car, get all our guns ready. We can grab our food on the way. Let's sit down and enjoy a nice meal. Being that it is now almost 09:00AM, I am sure you two have worked up quite the appetite." Braden responded.

Braden walked out of the room. Marie and I put on our clothes. I can't help but get this bad feeling out of my stomach, but I didn't mention it. We have a good vibe going on, and I don't want to ruin it. I am sure it is just pre murder jitters, right? We all start loading up the car, putting our pistols tucked into our pants. Well, Marie did some sort of magic for hers in which it basically just disappeared in her hand. We packed the rifles in individual travel bags where they were already assembled and just the ammo to be loaded. We go over the plan once again to ensure everyone is on board and on track. I feed Ginger, fill up her water bowl. I put down some bones for treats and toss a couple of her favorite toys so she won't be bored while we are gone.

09:15AM, we are sitting down at our local breakfast diner. We all decided on the same thing to eat, a nice big breakfast burrito. They make them very large, so I doubt any of us will finish them. It comes with a choice of meat (we all decided on the bacon), eggs, hash brown, cheddar cheese, salsa, topped with country gravy. I would be a lot more excited to be eating this if we weren't going to do what we were about to do. We all sat there in silence as we picked at our burritos. We all drank at least two cups of coffee. I looked at the time and saw that it was now 09:35AM.

"Ok guys, let's get this show on the road." I said with hesitation.

No one answered. They just looked up at me, nodded, and got up. No one took their left overs. Our tab was $47.66, and I put down a hundred-dollar bill. We just got up and walked out, ready to meet our destiny. Whatever that may be...

chapter 14

We drive up and park two blocks down. I turn off the car and pop the trunk. We are all silent still, but get out of the car and go to the trunk. I get my bag that holds my weapon. Braden grabs his. It is time to get this shindig started.

I look at Marie, "Ok Marie, it's go time. Remember to stay to the right so I can have a clear shot at Silas in the doorway. If I miss or he somehow doesn't get hit, make sure you shoot him in the back of the head. Be careful, we can do this, and I love you."

"I love you too Mark, we can do this."

It's funny because we are already saying I love you. I don't know why, but it just feels right. The first day we met at the store, I felt like I could have said that to her. I look at Braden and give him a nod; he does the same. I give Marie a kiss and as she turns around to walk away; I smack her ass and give it a little squeeze. She turns her head and winks with a grin. We all start moving to our positions. I get across the parking lot, directly opposing Silas' door. I look over to my right and see Braden loading his rifle. I look forward and see Marie starting towards his door, moving slowly, so she gives us enough time.

My heart is beating faster than I think it ever has. So much of our future, my future, the town's future resides at this moment in time that is happening. I am watching Marie walk towards the door through my scope. It is as if it is happening in slow motion. Marie gets to the door; she looks in my direction with a worried look on her face. She gives a half smile, takes a deep breath and turns back forward. Marie lifts her hand up and slowly knocks on the door. A few seconds go by, which seems like an hour. The door starts to creek open slowly.

Silas is now at the door; however, he stands right in front of Marie. She is attempting to move out of the way to give me a shot, but it's not working. He keeps himself out of the way, shit. I am waiting for the perfect shot; however, it doesn't seem to present itself. It was almost as if he knew this was going to be happening. I am assuming Braden doesn't have a shot either. He is not taking any either way. I look in his direction, but I don't see him anymore. Shit, hopefully this takes a turn for the better.

I resume to watch the door from the scope. I see Silas put his hand out. Marie turns her head and looks at me in sheer and utter terror. Shit, we are made. Silas looks directly at me and waves, then blows a kiss. He signals me to come toward them; I comply. Carrying my rifle, aiming in their direction. When I get close enough to them, I say, "Hi Silas, we meet again."

"Mark, you have to know this was a terrible idea?"

"Seems alright with me. I have a few tricks up my sleeve."

"Oh, that friend of yours over there? No, that's taken care of. Just look."

I look over in the direction of where Braden was supposed to be hiding. I see him walking out from behind some cars. There he is. Wait what? There is someone behind him. A woman, she has her arm raised directly behind his back. She is most definitely a witch too. Fuck, we are fucking fucked. This other witch changes everything.

Braden yells, "Mark, we got a problem here. I have some company."

"I see that Braden. Just do as she says. We lost." I replied.

I look back to Marie and Silas. He is looking at me with a devilish grin.

"Mark, Braden, this is one of my wives. Her name is Blair. Say high Blair." Silas says with a satisfied tone.

Blair waves at us, and gives an exaggerated

wave and smile towards Marie. I have no idea what we are going to do here.

Marie looks at me with complete sadness in her eyes, "Mark, we lost. I have to go back with them. This is it. I was so lucky to of met you. I fell in love with you. That is why I will walk away and save your lives."

At that moment, something sets off in my head. I am not caring about any consequences. I drop my rifle and open up into a full sprint towards Silas and Marie. Silas claps his hands with little effort as if it annoyed him he had to clap. I hear Braden scream. I turn my head around and can't believe what I am seeing.

Braden is floating up in the air, looking like he is crucified on thin air. I see Blair is now doing movements with her hands and chanting. She throws one hand up while the other is still in front of her. I see Braden's index fingers snap backwards, touching the back of his hand. Blair makes another quick movement with her hand; Braden's pinky fingers snap to the sides of his hands. They look as if they are barely hanging on by a thread of skin.

Braden is screaming in agony. A sound you would never expect to hear from a grown man. But that amount of pain with bringing out the sounds we didn't know we can make. I turn to Silas and beg for him to make Blair stop; he puts up his hand, so she pauses. Braden does not come down, but the pain has stopped for a second.

"Ok, Mark, what's it going to be?" Silas said, "I am a fair man. We can work this out. How about you let me go on my way? I will take Blair and Marie with me. I will heal your friend over there. You will never have a witch problem again in your little town. How does that sound?"

"Silas, I can't let you take her from me. Marie has given me a new purpose in life. There is something special between us." I responded.

"I am sad that you have chosen this route. You are just going to have to watch your friend die. Then, afterwards, you will suffer worse than he did."

Silas had put down his hand and nodded to

Blair to continue. I also felt as if they had strapped me with something to hold me in place. Facing Braden, I am going to have to see something terrible. Just then, Blair smiles real big, and starts up with her casting again. Braden's middle and ring fingers skin peel off. Now there is bone showing for those two fingers. Blood is dripping all over the ground below him. It is starting to puddle up.

Silas says, "Don't worry Mark, I am keeping him awake and alive for as long as this takes to make sure he feels it all."

Braden's left arm now curls towards his right shoulder. His hand is now making a gun gesture like everyone does when they are kids with the index and middle finger pointing and the thumb straight up. His thumb goes down like making a shot, however a real gunshot sound is made. Braden screams, and I can see that the first digit of his bare middle finger has shot into his shoulder. His thumb rises and drops twice more, repeating the last two digits of the bare bone lodging into his shoulder.

His left are returns to the crucified position. Braden's right arm now repeats the shooting of finger digits into the opposing shoulder. Braden is no longer screaming. He is just staring into nothingness. I am sure he is in shock at this point; I hope he no longer feels anything. Braden's lower jaw now opens excessively. I could hear his jaw breaks as it opens. All of his teeth immediately fly out of his mouth and align in a straight line in front of his face. Blood pour's out of his mouth. I can see his eyes open wider than they have ever opened. His ring fingers from both hands bare bones digits dis-attach from his hands. The bones tap onto the teeth and start to play the tune of the *Halloween* movie theme.

The audacity of these two, to just play with someone's life and make a mockery of it. I can tell there can't be much life left in Braden. I am pretty sure they notice this as well. At that moment, Braden's close rip off of him. Next is the rest of his skin. He is now just a body of muscle, organs, and bones. His intestines start to move out and wrap around his neck. This is where his body drops and is hung from his own intestines. Braden's body is now completely lifeless. I guess this means it will be my turn.

I still don't have control over my body. After witnessing that atrocity of what might be the most heinous act of murder, I am in shock and not sure I could move if I tried to. My body is forcefully turned around by Silas. I now notice that I am floating above the ground, not high, not like Braden, only an inch or two. I look at Silas, who has a grin, as if that made him happier than ever.

"Mark, did you enjoy the show? That Blair has a genuine talent for being creative. Wouldn't you say so?" Silas said. "I will tell you what Mark, I am feeling generous. I do want Marie to be happy. I am planning on making her one of my wives too. How could I not? Just look at her. So to make her happy, I won't kill you. As long as you get on your knees, kiss my bare toes, beg for mercy, and tell me I am your god. Ok?"

"Fuck you." I say under my breath.

"What did you say Mark, I hope you accept, otherwise I won't be playing nice. If I have to make Marie even more upset because of this, you will get it worse than Braden. So what was that again?"

I scream at the top of my lungs, "FUCK YOU SILAS! YOU'RE A CUNT!"

Silas just looks at me, and I see his grin slowly change to a frown. He shakes his head and walks towards me. Silas gestures his hand in a circular motion and I start to spin in a very slow circle. Marie cries and screams, "Silas, stop. You got what you wanted. You got me. Leave Mark alone or I will make your life a living hell."

Silas responds, "There's that fire I love about you. I can't wait to take that to bed. Help you work out some of that anger. Besides, you heard me Marie. I am a decent man. I offered him a way to live. A way he can escape his deathly fate."

"I am warning you Silas, if you hurt him, you will regret it."

"Let's be real here Marie. What are you going to do? I am stronger than you. You couldn't hurt me if I was asleep."

Silas turns back towards me and lifts his hands to start his gestures and chants. I am still spinning and now my arms extend out to the crucified position. My legs are now opened into a wide stance. I can feel them all stretching that is hurting. It feels as if it was the beginning of getting quartered by horses. The stretching continues, and the pain is starting to really kick in. I start to wail in agony.

Marie screams, "ENOUGH."

I see Marie put her palms out, facing Silas. He looks like something is hurting his head and he grabs it like a sudden migraine has penetrated his brain. My pain has subsided in an instant and I drop to the ground. Blair notices what is happening, and she grabs a hold of me with her magic, locking me into place. Marie notices and throws up her palm at her has well. Blair folds over, holding her head as well. The distraction of Blair must have given a slight release from Silas, for he picks up his head and puts his hands out in what looks like Ryu from Street Fighter doing a haduken. Marie launches against the wall behind her and immediately falls to the ground, appearing to pass out on contact.

Silas now turns back to me and so does Blair. They are both smiling, knowing that they are about to inflict some real damage to me. They both put their hands up and I am once again locked into place, set to be quartered by invisible horses, it would seem.

The stretching sets in. I can hear the seams in my clothing start to break. Marie gets up and throws her palms out again. This time she has frozen both Silas and Blair. She put them in the crucifix position.

Silas says, "How the fuck are you doing this? I am more powerful than you. You shouldn't be able to bind me like this."

Marie does some more gesturing and raises her arms to the sky. Clouds roll in fast. It starts to pour rain, thunder. Marie is pissed, she walks right up to his face where his still can't move. He looks baffled by what is happening. Marie walks over to me and hugs and squeezes me.

Marie asks, "Are you ok?"

I respond, "I think so. Nothing hurts anymore."

"Good. I am going to hurt them, so I need you to keep your eyes closed."

"Fuck no, I want to see them suffer."

"This will only hurt them; I cannot kill them right now."

Marie lifts Silas and Blair into the sky. They are both suddenly struck with lightning. I can smell the rotting flesh from the electrical hit they took. They both launched across the parking lot. Denting the vehicles they slammed against. They don't appear to be dead, but they aren't moving yet. That is a plus, I guess. Marie holds my hand and then lightning struck them both again. Silas starts to get up and at that moment, we teleport to back home. We need to find a new hideout or something similar. We need to save this city. I guess we can stay here because he can find us anywhere. We really need to figure out a new plan.

chapter 15

Marie was walking around frantically. Pacing back and forth, mumbling to herself. Then something came to me that didn't occur to me until now.

"Marie, why didn't you use the gun on Silas?" I asked.

"Holy shit. I completely forgot I even had the gun. When I saw Blair was there too, I knew there was problems for us. Besides, Blair changes everything. They are so powerful together. The gun wouldn't have done anything at all." Marie answered.

"But we had a plan. Wouldn't the gun have killed Silas?"

"Yes, the gun would've killed Silas. But we would have pissed off Blair. If she had that kind of rage energy, she would've destroyed us. Destroyed the motel and everyone in it. Hell, she might have just erased the city off the map with that kind of fury."

"Ok, fuck. What are we going to do Marie? There's another witch with Silas now. They just killed Braden. But not killed him. They tortured him. They did some disturbing ass shit to him. Oh my god, holy fucking shit. I am just starting to comprehend. WHAT THE FUCK! I cannot believe what I just witnessed. That happened to Braden... How can we defeat them if they can do that? But... You. You overpowered them. How did you do that? You fucked them up magically."

"I know that was really bad what they did to Braden. I cannot believe I came from a coven that could do a thing like that. I don't know what

I did. My body took over when I saw they were going to harm you. I just knew I couldn't let them hurt you."

"Ok, maybe there is something to that. Like you said, if we killed Silas, Blair would get a powerful rage. Is that what happened with you?"

"I didn't think of it that way. I guess it was rage. Well, rage and love."

"That's good. Real good. Do you think you can harness that? I wonder if you can control it. Make it happen on the regular."

"I don't know. That was the first time that ever happened. I can try."

"Yes, you have to try that. Maybe just think about those things happening to me. See if you can conjure it up on your own. Without me actually in danger. I mean, you controlled the fucking weather. You made lightning strike them. Twice."

"Wow, holy shit. You are right. I did do that. How the fuck did I do that?"

"Well, I guess that's what we are here to find out. We need to get you prepared before they regroup and come after us. Or even worse, start to kill everyone in town."

"Yes... Yes, that is exactly what I need to do. I need to kill them both. That will save us all."

After we had conversed for a while, I started to realize we don't have a clue about what we are doing. This is uncharted territory. That scares the living daylights out of me. If Marie can't figure out how to control her powers, we might just be fucked. The other part to this is, she did not know she was that powerful. She is against the people who were supposed to teach her everything too. This is one really fucked up situation.

The one thing that I do know about Marie is she has determination. So with that, even if I am scared, I know she is going to figure this all out. Let's just hope she does before the town gets too bloody. I just hope I can play some part in this. I hope I can figure out a way to hide and be able to shoot one of them, or something that will not leave Marie to do all the heavy lifting herself. Who am I kidding though? She will be the one to do all of it.

I've never seen anything like what happened at the motel. She controlled the weather. She was able to block them out from doing anything to me, even though they had me in their grip already. It was truly incredible. Now I am going to have to try and figure out a way to help her harness this. How am I going to do that though? Not that long ago that I didn't even know that witches and magic were actually real.

chapter **16**

We spent the next few days trying to figure out ways for Marie to learn to harness her energy. One thing that I have come to understand and realize there is some true potential to it is meditation. There is something special to the Shaolin warrior monks who can do some crazy things by learning how to meditate and harness their energy, or qi as they call it.

This is the third day since the madness went down at the Robertson's motel. Marie is starting to get good at meditation. The first day, she couldn't sit still. She was fidgeting around. It was hard for her to try to release everything from her brain. To just allow, have no control as control. This is when I looked up ways to help get into a meditative state. Breathing appears to be everything.

We tried several breathing techniques to see which might help the most. In the end, the best way for Marie was to just breathe slowly. Counting as she breathes. Breathe in for a count of ten, hold for a count of ten, and then breathe out for a count of ten. Repeat over and over. She had some success being able to do a little more with her magic when she was in this state. Nothing like she did at the motel though. That could be a problem for us. I will keep that to myself though. Don't want to spread any doubt to her.

"Ok Marie, I want you to do your breathing, but this time I want you to imagine Silas and Blair are here in front of us. I want you to figure out how you were able to harness the weather and use lightning to strike as a weapon. Ok?"

"Easier said than done, Mark. I will continue to try though. I am pretty sure we have little time left before they call me back out. Then it will be go time."

"That's right Marie. We don't have a lot of time. But I know you can do this."

I put up a watermelon on my table in the back. I told Marie to try to harness the lightning again. To strike the watermelon. She tried and tried again. Over and over. At this point, it was too late in the day to continue. She needs to get some rest though. Being well rested is just as important as being prepared for the fight.

"It's ok Marie. There is always trying again tomorrow." I said while rubbing her shoulders, trying to comfort her.

"You don't need to save me. I know I am going to be taken out if I don't hone this energy and be able to harness the elements."

As she said that, I could see it in her eyes. Her eyes flashed, as if there was lightning inside her eyes.

"Yea Marie, you're right. If you don't hone this energy, they will take you out. Along with myself and everyone else in this town. Shit, I bet they even torture poor Ginger. So don't fuck this up Marie."

"What the fuck Mark? How are you going to talk to me like that?"

As she was responding, I could see her eyes flash brighter, more intense. There were black clouds rolling in. My plan had worked. If I said messed up things, it would piss her off and her anger and aggression is what harnessed this intense energy. Now, all she needs to do is figure out how to tap into that rage when she needs to.

"Marie, look up. It's working. See if you can make the lightning hit the watermelon."

Marie looked up. She saw that there were clouds and could hear the thunder. She focused in on the watermelon. The same way ginger would focus on an intruder, right before an attack. BOOM, the watermelon burst into nothing. There was just a large black circle in place of where the watermelon was, and my table was smoking. Somehow that didn't catch on fire.

"You fucking did it Marie! All it takes is to piss you off. So, when we see them, I don't think it will be that hard for you to do."

"Yes, I should be able to do that. The only problem is that the lightning won't be enough. They were able to withstand it last time. I will have to figure out something to finish them off."

"One step at a time. This was a big win. Let's just focus on that we... well, you accomplished this part of it."

"Ok, yeah, you're right. I have worked up quite the appetite though. Let's go to the store and get some food."

"Sounds good. Let's go."

Marie and I grabbed our things and head out the door to head to the market. This will be odd though. This is the first time going into the store knowing that I will never see Braden there again. Come to think of it, I wonder what everyone is thinking about him being gone. I tried to cover it up and text his manager from his cell phone. Saying that he is quitting because he needs to find himself and travel the world. Regardless, it will feel weird going into the store knowing that I covered up his murder.

We get to the store, and instantly I could tell there was something off. Much like the first time that I had run into Silas at the store. It was eerie out, like there was a certain heaviness in the air. One thing that I notice, there aren't very many cars in the parking lot. Another red flag. I am starting to get the feeling this is the day that Silas and Blair came out to play.

Marie and I walk through the front automatic doors. Instant regret. Although there is no one in sight. It appears that there is blood splattered everywhere. One of the worst parts is that we don't know where they are hiding. Silas and Blair could be anywhere. So now we are on high alert. Realizing today is the day. I look at Marie. "Time to show them what you're made of."

"I guess you're right Mark. It's now or never."

At that moment, I notice a head peek over

the top of the aisle in front of us. I see the face of a woman that works at the store. There's something odd about her face though. I try to focus on it and figure out what's different, besides the fact that she is looking over the top of a grocery store aisle. At that moment, her head floated up, and I realized there was nobody attached to the head. Her face was distinct because it was lifeless. Frozen, but frozen in a perfect smile.

I could see the blood dripping out of her neck. It had slowed down a bit, so it has obviously been dis-attached for a while. Then from one head now turned into three heads from people who worked at the store. All frozen into big smiles with blood dripping slowly out of the severed necks. They all start floating around, as if someone was juggling their human heads.

"What.... The.... Fuck...." I mumbled in disbelief of what I was seeing.

In the store, just to the left of the entrance, right next to me, there is a basketball hoop. Why does the store have this? They got it after the high school, won a basketball championship thirty years ago and left it. The woman's head is now thrown, well I guess invisibly thrown and made a perfect swish. Nothing but net. Her head falls to the ground next to my feet and her blood splashes me. The other two heads follow.

The headless bodies now walk out from the sides of the aisles. They appear to be dancing. Music comes on over the speakers in the store. It's *Thriller*. The bodies are now performing the music video dance. Silas has a real ridiculous sense of humor with no regard for human life. Marie and I have just been standing here in the entrance. Baffled and not understanding on what we should even be doing.

I feel like I am dreaming. Everything seems to move in slow motion. The bodies are moving in unison and probably better than they would have if they were still a part of the live individual that had inhabited them prior to death. There is something seriously wrong with the headless bodies now moonwalking away from us and back around the aisles. If this wasn't so disturbing, I would probably be impressed.

I look at Marie; I want to say something, but I can't find it within myself to speak. She is just looking around. She has a shocked look on her face. I can only imagine what she is trying to process, knowing she was supposed to be a part of the group that is doing these horrid things. We still haven't even seen Silas or Blair. That is just starting to process in my brain that we don't even know where they are to begin with.

The blood trails from the headless dancers appear to be moving. The blood puddles are forming into shapes now. I can't exactly tell what they are doing just yet. Oh wait, they are spelling out some words. It says, "You fucked up." Wow, this is just getting ridiculous with all the game playing they are doing.

Marie yells, "Cut the shit Silas. Come out here and face me. Bring your little bitch too."

Damn, Marie taking charge on this. I was getting nervous if she was going to freeze up with the look she had on her face. Appears she snapped out of it and has turned on her badass warrior witch mode. At that moment, all the lights shut off in the store. This can't be good. Ok, looks like Silas is putting on another Michael Jackson song. "Bad" starts playing and out comes Silas from around the aisle. He is wearing the infamous red leather jacket from the video. He is also doing the hand shaking like the video while being followed by the headless bodies with Blair coming up in the end as the caboose.

Silas, with a big smile says, "Eh, eh. How did I do? I have always wanted to re-enact those scenes. Come on, do I get an A+ performance or what?"

I yell, "What the fuck is wrong with you? How could you disrespect these people? How can you desecrate their bodies like that and make it into a joke? You are one fucked up piece of shit!"

"You better watch your tone with me little boy toy. You mean absolutely nothing to me." Silas snapped back with literal flames shooting out of his ears and his eyes turning completely red.

"In fact, I don't even care enough about you

to even lose my temper and kill you just yet. Marie seems to like you, so to make her happy when she comes back with me, I'll let you live. Doesn't mean I won't hurt you though."

Silas throws his right arm to his right and I fly across the store and land in the big box of watermelons. Ironically, where I met Marie for the first time. I smash into them and they get obliterated and spray watermelon juice everywhere.

Marie screams. I can just see above the cardboard box I am in, and her eyes actually flash like there is lightning inside them. She's pissed. She raises her hand and points it at them. Lightning erupts from her fingers and hits the headless bodies. They catch fire and disintegrate into ash within seconds. I see Blair raise her hand and the heads that are a few feet away from Marie levitate up and all smash into Marie. One hits her in the side, the next hits her in the shoulder, and the last bounces right off of her head. This knocks her a few feet.

Marie stands back up and makes a motion

like she was pulling something big towards herself. The whole isle falls forward, bouncing off of Blairs back. She lands face forward on the ground in front of Marie. She runs forward and soccer kicks Blair's face as if she was trying to score a goal. I literally saw a tooth of Blairs fly across the room. Blair falls limp to the ground. Marie lifts her foot, which she is wearing some nice Dr. Martin's boots, and repeatedly stomped on Blair's head. Blair's body was reacting to the first couple of stomps. Now it is just limp. There is also a pool of blood under her face. I am going to assume Blair is dead.

Marie looks up to see Silas standing and staring in disbelief. Silas raises his hands up and lets out a bellowing, "Whoa! Whoa! Was that really necessary, Marie? Did you have to kill my wife? You will definitely replace her after this. I will also make you pay. Best believe we will be doing fifty shades of fucked up."

Silas lifted both of his arms to his sides, with palms facing up. He then slams them down to his side. It was chaos. There were grocery items flying from every which direction. A pack of diapers here, a can of tomatoes there, a bottle of vinegar, and the list goes on. I try to sit up to get out and try to help, but I get nailed across the side of the head by a glass bottle of water. This nearly knocks me unconscious, but I am hanging in enough to tell Marie to run and save herself.

I am slowly fading; all I see is what looks like a tornado of canned vegetables along with spaghetti sauce swirling around in front of me. It is hard to open my eyes; they keep closing but I fight to open every time. I am seeing everything through a coat of crimson from all the blood now draining from multiple cuts on my head from the whirlwind of market madness. Lightning flying through the air, alcohol bottles exploding midair and the liquor catching fire. I feel as if I am witnessing an episode of Game of Thrones in front of me. There is an insane battle happening between two powerful beings and I am caught in the crossfire. Then, I see a thirty-two pack of water bottles flying straight at me. It lands directly on my head. I turned my face, so it didn't break my nose, but everything went lights out after the collision. Darkness.

chapter 17

Opening my eyes, completely confused about where I am. I am no longer in the grocery store. I look around with my eyes. Not moving my head, my neck hurts too much. Wait, I know these walls. I am home, in my bed. What the fuck just happened? How did I get here?

"Mark, finally, you are awake. I was getting worried. Let me get you a healing elixir; you will be good as new."

"Marie, what happened? Last I remember

was you were having an insane battle with Silas. There was fire, product tornadoes, head smashed Blair, moon walking headless workers. Is this real life?"

Marie walked back into the room with a cup full of pungent smelling liquid.

"Drink this Mark, I know it smells bad, but it will fix you right up."

I squeeze my nostrils closed with my left hand and grab the cup with my right. Down the hatch, it all goes. Looks like taking all those shots over the years served a purpose. I cough a little and throw the cup out the door.

"Was that necessary to throw the cup, Mark?"

"Fuck yes it was. That stuff tasted horrible. I know it will make me feel better, but throwing the cup made me feel better about drinking it."

"That doesn't make any sense."

"I know it doesn't, but I don't care. Anyway, please tell me what the fuck happened after I got knocked out last night."

Marie jumped onto the bed and sidled up next to me.

"Well, as you said, I was in an epic battle with Silas. After he sent that pack of water bottles at you and knocked you out. I lost it. I thought he killed you. The amazing thing is, I basically turned into a giant ball of lightning. I ran straight at him. He tried to send objects at me. They disintegrated when they touched the giant orb around my body. I got up to him and threw a punch at his face. I hit him and he flew back and went through the wall of the grocery store. The bad thing is the store caught on fire. It burnt to the ground. I went over to you and teleported you to where you are now. I went in search for Silas after so I can finish the job and kill him. As the entire store burned down, I searched everywhere. He somehow escaped. I know I hurt him badly. The only problem now, he will figure out a way to neutralize my new found lightning power. I will need to figure out another way to attack. But for now, I just want to nurse you back to health."

"Wow Marie, you are a legit badass. How can Silas handle that kind of force? That's fucking scary."

"He's been around for a long time. He is very powerful. One thing that's good is that I killed Blair. He won't be as strong if there isn't another witch to link to him."

"Well, I guess that is a start. Hey, I just thought of something. What is going to happen with the rest of the town people? There are several that have died and the local market has just been burned down. There doesn't seem to be much of a reaction from everyone."

"They are all under somewhat of a trance. As much as Silas wants to pretend he is a badass, he doesn't want to get caught. That will always cause another witch hunt, like the Salem trials. I mean, they were completely wrong with their accusations. But we definitely don't want to go through that again."

"What do you mean they were wrong with their accusations? Don't tell me you were there during that time. Wasn't that like three hundred years ago?"

"Yes, they were, and no I wasn't. Silas was, though. He was there and said that the people of Salem were just accusing women and men of being witches to further their political agendas. Any woman who spoke up for herself or didn't just do as she was told, accused of witchcraft. Meanwhile, the actual witches just watched and laughed."

"Wait, Silas is over three hundred years old? Dare I ask how old you are?"

"Yes, I think he's somewhere in the four hundred year range. Don't worry about me, I am actually twenty-two. I haven't lived long in comparison of them. They found me and took me in at a young age. My birth family had abandoned me. Then, the coven found me; they said they could feel a strong power from me and took me in. They taught me witchcraft, which is why I can do all that I can do now. I couldn't complete the full transformation though. Now that I think about it, I killed Blair. That might be why I was able to summon that type of power. I made a sacrifice, so now I have my full power.

Holy shit. I don't even really know what this means. Apparently, I can summon the power of lightning."

"No offence, but I am thrilled that you aren't really old. But that leaves me the question of what is going to happen to us? I know we just got together, but if I am going to age and you are not...What does that mean in the future? Can I convert to a witch or something? I might be thinking too far ahead, but I love you."

"Mark, I love you. You are a genius. If you become a witch, or men are also called warlocks, whatever doesn't really matter. If we create our own coven together, we can link ourselves. I will become more powerful. I can't really teach you anything right now, but the power bond will be there."

"Ok, wow, that sounds awesome. What do I have to do?"

"There is a blood ritual we have to do; we can do it tonight. Luckily, it's a full moon. I will get it all prepared. For now, rest, get some sleep. This is going to be powerful."

chapter 18

t was around **10:30PM**, Ginger woke me up, licking my face. Shit, I forgot to feed her dinner. Wow, I feel like I am completely healed. That elixir really did the job, apparently. I better go feed Ginger, poor dog. I walk downstairs and grab Gingers bowl. I realize I forgot to get more kibble, so looks like Ginger is eating a nice big steak tonight. I cut it up into some pieces and toss the raw meat into her bowl. Wow, she ate that fast!

Marie comes in the front door and walks

right up to me with a big smile. First, she pets Ginger on the head, then she comes to me and gives me a big kiss.

"Mark, are you ready? I am so happy. I never thought you would want to go on this journey like this. I was getting really sad thinking that one day, I was going to live on and you were going to be old and die."

"Well, this is all fairly new to me. What you just said to me sounds insane. I barely even knew witchcraft even existed not that long ago. Honestly, I wouldn't want it any other way, though. You mean everything to me."

"Mark, you are the sweetest. We are going to go to my hideout in the woods. This is going to be a process. Just remember, there is no going back after this. So you will need to be certain that this is what you want. It will bond us for life."

"Marie, there is nothing I would want more."

I get dressed and right before I was about to eat some food, Marie said I couldn't eat anything. I needed to be in a fasted state, and I need to take some sort of other concoction now before we head out to where our ceremony will take place.

I drink the whole concoction and put on my shoes. Time to head out to the middle of the woods. Marie said she will drive because there is a good chance I will hallucinate. As we are driving, I notice that all the lights are starting to leave a trail behind them. As if the headlights are drawing lines; this reminds me of the time I went to the store with my friends after I took psilocybin mushrooms. Which turns out they are a part of the concoction. Go figure.

We get to the end of a street, that I am not even sure where we are, and go off roading. We are driving down a dirt road that eventually turns into just woods surrounding us. I do not know how Marie knows where we are going, there are no demarcations, just thick woods. After driving deep into the forest for what seemed like a half an hour, we finally stop. Marie gets out and I follow.

Marie walks up to this overgrown bush and stands right in front of it. She puts her things down, closes her eyes, and does some sort of hand gestures while whispering some chants. The bush then disappears, or more so turns into some sort of doorway that leads to a path. We walk through the entrance and when I look back to see the other side; the bush was already back. Talk about an awesome hidden pathway that no one would ever figure out.

As we continue down the pathway, I notice we are coming up to some dim light. When we finally get to the end of the pathway, there is a perfect circle cut out of the deep wilderness. There appears to be a total apartment looking place here. It's all out in the open, but there is a toilet, a sink, even what looks like a refrigerator. I guess you really can have everything with witchcraft. In the center of everything, there is a circle of black candles, all lit. There appears to be some sort of alter in the center of the candles. There is a plethora of herbs amongst other things set in wooden bowls in-between the candles.

Marie is going around making everything is

in place. I notice there is a large bowl sized cauldron also in the middle of it all. There is even wood placed underneath it to heat. Next to the cauldron, there is a large knife, Damascus steel. Looks like it's just about time to get this shindig started.

"Ok Mark, it's time. Are you ready?"

"I am a little nervous, but I am excited."

"It is very important you follow my lead. I will say things I need you to repeat. Don't worry, I will tell you when, but please pay attention."

"Yes, I will Marie. Let's do this already."

At that moment, Marie snapped her fingers, and a large flame came barreling from under the caldron. I kneel down in front of it. Marie walked up directly behind me, pressing her body onto my back lightly. She is now directing different plants and herbs, among other things, into the cauldron. I see a few stones and crystals float into there. I am pretty sure I just saw a tongue and some other animal organs go in as well.

Marie raises her hands up. Tell's me here is when I repeat what she says and starts speaking with authority, "I call upon the Guardians of the Watchtower of the North."

"I call upon the Guardians of the Watchtower of the North."

"I call upon the Guardians of the Watchtower of the East."

"I call upon the Guardians of the Watchtower of the East."

"I call upon the Guardians of the Watchtower of the South."

"I call upon the Guardians of the Watchtower of the South."

"I call upon the Guardians of the Watchtower of the West."

"I call upon the Guardians of the Watchtower of the West."

"I call upon you to create a union. To make two into one."

"I call upon you to create a union. To make two into one."

"I take the power of the earth, I take the power of the air, I take the power of fire, I take the power of water, and I sacrifice my power to join as one."

Marie walks to the cauldron and grabs the blade, she slices the palm of her left hand and squeezes what seems to be a lot of blood into the boiling assortment of natural commodities. She then walks to me and hands me the blade telling me to do the same as she did.

"I take the power of the earth, I take the power of the air, I take the power of fire, I take the power of water, and I sacrifice my power to join as one."

I the slice the palm of my left hand and squeeze as much blood out as I can. The flame now roars and engulfs the cauldron. I stumble back and I feel Marie put her hand on my back to steady me.

"Mark, they are happy with your sacrifice. This means you will be accepted and we can join as one. We just need to finish the ritual. Take off all of your clothes."

"What? Right now? Ok."

Marie ripped off her clothes as if she was a professional wrestler about to get into the ring. I was a little stunned by the sight of her doing that; Marie noticed I was not taking my clothes off and waved her hand at me and all my clothes flew off my body like they were never even on me to begin with. She walks to the giant black pot, and the flames simmered down. She put both of her hands into the bubbling liquid and scooped out some with cupped shaped hands and drank the dark red sludge. She signaled to me to do the same. I was scared to put my hands in, but I knew I had too, anyway. I dipped them in, and to my surprise, it did not hurt at all. I lift the content and drink the odd feeling and tasting concoction.

I could feel it surging through my body. It was like nothing I had ever felt before. There was an energy flowing in my veins, a power that felt incredibly strong. I look at Marie wondering if this was all we had to do, wondering why we had to get naked to drink our brew. She must have noticed that was what I was thinking and shook her head with a smile while proceeding to speak.

"Thank you, Guardians of the Watchtowers,

for allowing our union. For joining us and blessing us with the power of the elements, and allowing us to serve you. As above, so below."

Marie then pulls me over to the cauldron and reaches her hand in and starts to spread the warm, crimson liquid all over my body. She puts my hand in and puts my hand onto her body. We do this until we cover each other's bodies entirely. Face, hair, literally every centimeter of our bodies. She then takes me to an open patch of dirt and lays me down on my back. She now kneels down and drifts her chest from my abdomen up to my chest and kisses me.

Marie then moves her legs up and mounts me. This time, it's different. It isn't just sex, it s love making. There is genuine passion. This is the very essence of love making. As she is riding me, rain pours onto us. Lightning, thunder, and wind blowing everywhere. It is as if all the elements are joining us and comforting us as we are sealing our union.

There is an energy that is flowing around us, through us as one. A circle sets ablaze around us.

The rain isn't even affecting the flames, and the weird thing is the water isn't even cold, it feels warm. In amazement, I look around and it is as if everything is moving in slow motion. I look into Marie's eyes; I see actual flames inside with what looks like bolts of lightning.

After climax, in which the surrounding flames must've shot up at least fifteen feet high. Marie lays down next to me where we fall asleep looking up at the stars. All the surrounding craziness continues throughout the night. It doesn't bother at all though; it is as if we are all now as one. Actually, we are now as one.

chapter 19

The sun is shining on our faces as I wake from the natural light. I feel almost in disbelief at what had just happened. Was that real? Did I just become a witch? Or warlock? Or whatever you call it. I just lay there in the dirt, moving my eyes around. I am still confused. I don't feel any different. It almost felt like that was a dream. Was it a dream? It couldn't have been. I am still laying naked in the dirt with Marie next to me.

I sit up trying to get a grip on what is going

on. I look at Marie; she is still sleeping but fidgeting around a little. Ok, I am going to stand up and find my clothes. Hopefully, there is some water. I'm so thirsty I feel like I have never had water in my life. I stand up and I instantly regret it. I feel so dizzy; the world is spinning fast around me. I walk to grab ahold of anything I can but I stumble. I manage to walk to a nearby tree and hold on to it.

My face feels hot. I can feel all the blood rushing to it. My hands go cold. I feel the cold sweats starting to take over my body. There is an uneasy feeling in my stomach. A queasiness that feels as if there is sludge starting to slowly crawl up my esophagus. I am losing control over my body and I buckle down to one knee. I feel as if I am swaying the way a fishing boat does when getting hit by small waves. I lean my head forward and throw up.

Hurling anything that might have stayed in my stomach. My body is tensing and wrenching. I feel as if I am getting a full-body workout at the same time. Suddenly, I feel Marie's hand on my back. Sliding it up and down my spine.

Marie says, "I'm sorry Mark. I should've warned you not to get up too fast. This happens to the best of us. Let me heal you and fix you right up."

"I don't care, do whatever you have to do. Just make it stop."

Marie rubs her hands together as if she was trying to start a fire with the friction. She has a mantra, or spell she is saying and she puts her hand onto my back. Within seconds, I have a cooling sensation flow through my body. It feels as if she opened up my back, poured in cool water in my veins and it traveled throughout my body.

"I feel great now. How did you do that? That was amazing."

"Mark, you can do that too now. You can do so much. All of my powers, you can now access. I am stronger as well. You will have some bond with a specific element that will be powerful as I do with lightning. It will take time and patience to learn. This is a long process; we will have all the time in the world as long as we can get rid of Silas."

"Fuck, I almost forgot about him. Last night was incredible. I feel so alive now. Like nothing I have ever felt before. Does this feeling stay? Or does it fade after a while?"

"Mark, you are going to feel good like this all the time. As long as you follow my lead, give thanks to all the elements. We will have rituals we perform together. Our bond is going to be so strong, our bond to the earth, moon, sun, and stars will also be so powerful. Our opportunities will be endless."

"Wow. I knew from the first time that I saw you that I had been drawn to you. I didn't know why, but I now believe it was destiny to meet you. To fall in love with you. Nothing has ever felt so perfect. Any chance you have anything to eat out here? I am famished now that I have thrown up everything that was in my stomach."

"Yes, I will make us some food. How does a breakfast burrito sound?"

"Sounds fantastic. Any chance we can get our

clothes back on? Well... I would like my clothes on. You don't have to if you don't want to. I am enjoying the view."

Marie giggles and looks at me and snaps her fingers. We are both now clothed with the clothes we were wearing yesterday. They are no longer dirty or ripped, as if they were freshly bought and never even worn.

"I could definitely get used to this. Seems like the sky is the limit."

"There are no limits, Mark. The possibilities are endless now."

Marie serves the burritos and sits on the ground next to me. I am enjoying what we have going on right here, but I also have a pit in my stomach thinking about Silas. How can he possibly be so strong to withstand the magical beating he received? I can't believe how old he is. He has wisdom and magical strength that is unmatched. We will need to really figure out what we are going to do.

"Marie, we need to get back home. We have to figure out a plan of action. We will have to outsmart Silas. We have our magical union as a boost of strength, but we still need to figure out our plan. Besides, I am sure Ginger is freaking out right now."

"Ok Mark, let's finish up eating and grab some of this stuff. There are different things we can grab so I can make some concoctions and hopefully neutralize his power."

"Sounds good. Just tell me what to get and where it is and I will be your harvester."

Marie gives me a list of things to grab. It is a lot more than I expected to be grabbing, but I grab it all anyway without question. I realized I won't make any sense of what her answer would be, anyway.

We grab all of our things. Marie had some bags lying around so we can do it all in one trip. Our car isn't the closing thing to get to. We take all the bags and take our trip to the car and put them all in the trunk. I have this extra energy flowing through me now, so everything feels brand new to me. Walking, the touch of the dirt, the feeling of the car door on my hand, it is like being a baby again and experiencing everything again for the first time.

As if she was reading my mind, Marie then let me know about the heightened awareness and feelings I will be experiencing. The other thing that was heightened as well was the pit in my stomach, caused by Silas. I feel terrified. This is a powerful being. He wants to kill Marie and I.

I guess this is the point where we will just have buckle up and figure out what the fuck we can do.

chapter 20

We arrive at my house and bring in all the items that we had grabbed from Marie's hideaway spot. I still have a level of euphoria from the magical transformation I had just went through. I still don't even really know what that even means for me. Other than that I will now live a long, long life with Marie, well, if we survive that is. I couldn't be happier about having this experience with her though. She has changed my life and have given me purpose.

Ginger come bouncing around as we start to settle in and get everything out of the bags, setting them on the dining table. I feel bad that I haven't had the time to spend with Ginger and give her the proper attention she deserves. I guess when this is all over, if I am still alive maybe the three of us will take a road trip and enjoy the great outdoors.

Marie has turned my dining table into what looks like a science lab. There are burners, beakers, amongst many other things I don't know. At this point, I am feeling a little run down, overwhelmed. Marie said that it was normal to feel like that after my transformation. I went to my bathroom and turned on the shower. I wanted to take a nice long, hot shower. I sit down and let the water run on my head; in which I get into a meditative like trance.

During my time sitting here, I felt something. My body has a sensation that I can't quite explain. I could feel a certain level of connection to the water. It was almost electrifying. As if the water had consciousness and was communicating with me through the absorption of my body. It was intense.

I started to see visions. It was things that I couldn't quite understand what was happening. It was wilderness; almost as if I was in the body of a bird flying through the forest. It was amazing! I could feel it, the wind on my face as I glided around. Then it shifted to another scenery. Like leaping from one entity to another. This time I was carrying on throughout the town of Forestdale. I could see the construction of the market. It appeared to be ahead of schedule somehow; I am sure Marie had something to do with that. I felt as if I was the actual wind now. I was moving fast, but it seemed as if I was in slow motion at the same time.

It appeared to be I was doing some sort of remote viewing. At first, it seemed like I had little control and just had to go with the flow. I had an idea though. I wondered if it was possible to steer my consciousness into directions I wasn't already going. Maybe, just maybe, I might be able to control what I see. I can try to use this to my advantage.

Being that I know the town like the back of my hand, I was going to attempt to carry my wind like viewing to the Robertson's motel. As I put my focus on turning to the right direction. I start to shift towards there. Excited, I continue to emphasize my focus on just getting to the motel first. I am doing it; I am actually controlling myself, or whatever you would call what I am right now. It feels like I am in the scene from "Evil Dead" where the camera view is flying through the air, only much slower. It is truly surreal.

I make my way to the Robertson's motel. Remembering what Silas had said the first time we met, I knew he was in room thirty one. Well I hoped he was in the same room and too arrogant to change rooms or motels. As I reached the room, I felt cautious about being that close to him. He is the high priest, after all. I would imagine he could probably sense me or feel my presence, so I really wanted to take it easy. This is my first time trying to spy on an all-powerful being.

I hear Silas inside his room. However, I can tell that there is something off here. He must be speaking to others from the coven. I do my best to stay undetected as I flow my way through a crack in the window. This might be the weirdest thing I have ever done. I am astral standing in the room, just floating or whatever it is in the corner of the room.

Silas is on the bed, still talking on the phone. He is indeed speaking to someone from the coven. He is telling them that Blair is dead; he hasn't secured Marie, and that he plans to burn the town to the ground just to spite her at this point. He laughs a little and then says he plans on attacking Marie at the dumbasses house. I am the dumbass. He proceeds to insult me and say derogatory things about Marie and what he plans on doing to her once he has taken her back and weds her. Then, he drops the bomb, Silas says, "I am going to rest for three days. On the fourth day I will go to his house and burn this whole mother fucking town to the ground."

I react, I move back a little. My emotion must've strengthened my spirit. I actually moved the curtain. It was slightly done, but it caught his eye. He stands up and walks his way towards where I am standing. Panicking, I move away from the curtain. The only problem is that Silas is now in-between me and the window. I can try to stay calm and when he moves out of the way, I will make my exit then. I am getting really nervous though; I don't even really know how I got here to begin with. I don't know if he can sense me or hurt me if he finds me somehow. This is all new and might be one of the scariest predicaments I have ever been in.

Silas is still patiently looking at the curtain area. You can tell he is pondering something. Hopefully, he can't figure out that I am here though. Saved by the door; someone knocks and it occupies his attention. He peeks out the window. His takeout has arrived. Before he heads to the door, he reaches into his pocket. He pulls out what appears to be some sort of dust or sand like substance. He whispers some words over it, then throws it back to the room.

Unfortunately for me, it hits me. It burns, like I was hit with acid. He must've suspected there was someone in the room. I don't let out any noises, but it's painful. After what seemed like an hour he started walking towards the door. I quickly flow through the window. I start towards my home, in what feels like supersonic speed. The moment I get home, I go inside and immediately to my body in the shower where I was still sitting.

The only difference is that where I was hit with the dust, I could see speckles of blood dripping out of my skin. Not really knowing what to do in this situation, I figure jumping into my body is my best bet of trying to connect back to it. I jump into my meat suit and wake up. Feeling like I am taking a deep breath for the first time after being under water for three minutes, I try to catch my breath.

I yell as loud as I can, "MARIE, HURRY COME HERE!"

Marie runs in as fast as she can. She opens the

shower door and sees me sitting. She notices the blood and says, "Mark, why the fuck are you bleeding?"

"I got into a trance, I think I was astral traveling or remote viewing or whatever it's called. I went to Silas' motel room. He threw some dust on me and it feels like I was burned with acid. HELP!"

"Oh shit. You must've tipped him off somehow, it's ok. I have something for that."

Marie quickly runs out the door and returns with several leaves in her hands. She puts them in her mouth and starts chewing them up. She then removes the chewed up leaf and spreads it out across a wound. She continues to do this until she covers all the wounds.

"Marie, what is this? What is it you are doing? Why did you chew it up?"

"This is a plantain poultice. You have to chew it up so the saliva helps break it down for the healing properties. Now I am going to wrap it with this flannel to hold it in place to heal."

"There is a lot to learn about all this, isn't

there?"

"Don't worry, young grasshopper, you will have all the time in the world to learn it."

As much as it was comforting to hear her say this, knowing that we aren't certain of our futures just yet. We have a very deadly, powerful warlock that wants us, well me dead. It is going to be kill or be killed in four days.

"Marie, when I was there, I heard Silas talking to someone on the phone. He said that he was going to come to my house in four days and burn the whole town down just to spite you. He plans on killing me, and taking you back to wed you."

"Holy shit Mark. You are a genius."

"Not the response I thought I would get, but ok. Can you please tell me what you mean?"

"You just found out his plan. He doesn't know that we know. He wasn't sure if someone was there with him. That is why he threw the astral dust. You must have hidden yourself good after that, you should've appeared to him or made a noise loud enough to hear. He would've killed you on the spot if he found you."

"Fuck, he could've seen me or heard me? I made sure to stay quiet, but I didn't think he could see me. Glad I held my composure."

"Now we can plan ahead, set traps and see what we can do to hopefully get an edge on him when he comes in four days. We got a lot of work ahead of us. Get some rest, heal, and we get started tomorrow."

"Ok, I am feeling better, this stuff feels like it is working like a miracle. I am going to go lay down now and rest though, love you, Marie."

"Love you."

Marie gave me a kiss and left the room while I laid down. Thinking about it, I must have been in that shower and astral traveling for a long time. I have no idea how it's night time already.

Chapter 21

hree more days. I am feeling much better. That poultice Marie made healed me up fast. I can't believe that our world has magical plants that can heal us. Most people don't even realize this, but the medicine in the earth is all around us. I am really excited to learn about this all after being healed so fast naturally. Marie even told me that the magic is in the plant. She did not use any powers this time.

I hop out of bed, feeling amazing compared to yesterday. All the wounds that were on my body are pretty much gone too. It doesn't even look like I was injured at all. Incredible. I am eager to find out what it is we are going to do. Hopefully Marie has some sort of plan; or at least an idea of a plan she wants to make.

We have three days to plan, and set up any type of trap we might set. I go into the kitchen and see Marie still frantically working at the table with her lab. Thinking about it, I woke up to an empty bed and realized that Marie probably hasn't slept yet. That can't be good.

I ask, "Marie, have you slept yet?"

Startled not realized I entered the room, Marie responds, "No, no I haven't yet."

"Shouldn't you get some rest? You need to be well rested and strong if we are going to go head to head with Silas, right?"

"I suppose you are right. I just want to get these concoctions going first. I am making some weapons and it will take a day for it to finish."

"What are you making?"

"I am making a few things. First one I am extracting the toxins from the Spotted Water

Hemlock plant. It is deadly if ingested. So I am going to make it concentrated and put it in a super soaker to hopefully get into his eyes and mouth. With it being concentrated, it might do the job on its own. Second, I am making a topical oil out of Jimson Weed. I want to fill a syringe or something like that. When it is injected into Silas, he will have many problems. Especially because I am making sure this is going to be very concentrated. What this can do is make him hallucinate, as well as give him hypothermia and tachycardia. Between the two of those, he should be in some real bad shape and at that point we can stab him in the heart and cut off his head."

"I hope it works out that easily. Sounds like we just need to figure out the best ways to rig them up to where he can walk into them."

"Yes, we can rig the doors and windows. We have to be real craft about it though. He can do some crazy things. The extractions will keep running on their own now. I am going to get some sleep."

"Ok, what should I do?"

"Eat, play with Ginger, do whatever it would be if you never met me."

"Oh, wow, I wish you didn't talk like that. Besides, it's almost hard to remember what it was like to not have you in my life. Even though it hasn't been that long. I'll figure something out. Go get some rest."

Marie went off to the room to get some sleep. I walked around my house, looking at every doorway or window. Thinking about how or why we would rig the traps for that specific area.

I am sure we can use some magic to be able to rig them up so the super soakers will start shooting when Silas comes through the door. Maybe we can rig the syringes to be above the door. So that when someone enters the room, they drop, and the plunger pushes down. I guess these are things I will need to think of when Marie gets back up. I will take some mental notes to show Marie when she gets up though.

I decided I should take her advice and do some things that I might normally do. I go to the backyard and call Ginger outside. I grab her favorite ball to play with, which is a blue racquetball. They always bounce really well and go very far. I start talking to Ginger in that excitable voice everyone does when playing with their dog.

"You ready girl? Ready? Want to chase the ball? Are you going to run real fast?"

Ginger, getting fed up with me. She starts to bark and run around in circles. Not being able to handle the anticipation, she starts to jump up and down. It wasn't till that point that I threw the ball for her. I threw it as far as I could to make sure she got a nice long run for it. I repeated these many times. Until the last time she comes back with the ball, she just drops it and lays down on the ground. I drop down to pet her and tell her she's a good girl. I walk over to the back door, where I keep dog treats. I walk back to Ginger and give her a handful of little bacon treats. This part of my day almost felt normal, before the magical madness.

chapter **22**

Two more days. I had turned in early last night. I wanted to make sure that I was taking the time and getting the proper rest. I definitely needed to make sure I was fully rested each day so I could perform at my highest potential. Marie and I both woke up at the same time. I look over at her, in which she was already staring at me. I smile really big and say, "Good morning beautiful."

"Good morning, handsome."

"I don't really want to get out of bed. I want

to lie here with you all day. Just stay right here. Not even doing anything. Just gazing into your eyes."

"Shut up Mark. You are too cute. I want to do the same, but we have a villain to kill."

"Nothing says love like plotting murder in the morning."

Marie jumps out of the bed and turns around and blows a kiss. I pretend to catch it, but sadly remember that I actually have to get out of the bed too. Reluctantly, I slowly roll out of the bed and drag myself to the kitchen. I immediately go to the Keurig and start making myself a latte.

I ask Marie, "Would you like a latte as well?"

"Is that even a question? I will start making some bacon and eggs."

"Music to my ears."

After making the coffee's, I pour a bowl of food for Ginger. She comes running at the sound of the food in her bowl and crashes into the wall with over excitement like she does every morning. I also crack the back door so she can go outside and do her business. I could get used to this kind of routine, just the three of us.

After eating breakfast, which we did outside, being that the dining table is currently a science lab of death. It was time to discuss on what we can do to set up my house to be a trap for when Silas comes. It is pretty hard to imagine what we can do to cover every window and door. With Silas' arrogance though, I highly doubt he would come through a window. He would want to be seen as he made a grand entrance through a door. Most likely the front door. Someone who pretends to have that much bravado would do nothing less.

I explain to Marie what I had thought of yesterday with rigging the super soakers to the doors and having the syringes above the door for a drop when he comes in. I also ask if that would be possible to set that up with magic. Marie says that it is possible to do just that, which is a relief. I also ask if there will be enough to have extra, just in case. I would like to have one of the super soakers on hand, as well as a syringe, amongst carrying a knife and a machete for good measures. Luckily there will be plenty.

Unfortunately, this is all becoming all too surreal. We will go to battle in my home nonetheless. It's almost weird to think of how I even got to this point in my life. Next thing, we will need to figure out where exactly are we going to be positioned. I will definitely have Ginger locked up in a room upstairs. Don't really want her to be hurt, or worse. I think I will position myself in a room downstairs, off to the side of the front door. That way, when he does come in, I want to see him suffering. Marie said she will be positioning herself just to the side of the door as well, but cloaking herself. As long as she doesn't move, she won't be seen. We have a fairly decent plan. It feels like there is something off with it though. I level of uncertainty.

We take the rest of the day getting the super soakers, syringes, and some other miscellaneous supplies from the store in the next town over. Can't be too careful in making sure we aren't being watched.

After we return from the store, we carefully

load them with their toxic contents. It's almost kind of funny that we are using a kid's water toy to implement death to a powerful supernatural being. One that could potentially destroy the world if he wanted to.

My mind has been running a mile a minute lately, thinking about all of this as well. I too, am now a supernatural being. I will learn to use magical powers, be able to live for a long, long time, I mean, be immortal really. That might be a hard thing to explain to my family and neighbors in fifty years when I look the same. I also wonder what other kind of beings are there? Maybe I will ask Marie another time. One step, one day at a time.

chapter 23

One more day. We are on the home stretch. Tomorrow will be the day that we go to war. I don't even know how to feel at this point. I am almost numb to it all. It is weird; I have a certain level of acceptance now. One that will just be ok with whatever the outcome is. I won't exactly have a choice in that, anyway. I will either be alive, or not.

So, I guess at this point I will just be. There has already been so much death and chaos in my town. From Braden being torn apart in front of us, to the grocery workers' bodies being used as puppets, as well as the store being burnt to the ground. How did it come to this point? Did all this happen just because I met Marie? Would this have happened regardless, or would she have gone to a new town and continued to run? There is no proper way to find out, but I do feel kind of guilty. I feel as if this might just be my fault.

What's done is done. I can't change the past. I can only live for the future. Whatever that future may be. I am looking forward to a future with Marie. Only one more day will decide our fates.

It has come time to eat lunch. After lunch will be when we start setting up the children's toys of mass destruction. After they are magically strung up, we won't be able to open the doors any more. So we need to get anything from outside the house done prior to that. We decide we are going to get pizza for lunch. We get our pizza with bacon, pepperoni, olives, jalapeños, and pineapples. That's right, pineapple is the best served on pizza. I am happy that Marie agrees as well. Nothing better than the spicy pepper with the sweetness. Ok, I am getting side tracked.

For fun, and some nostalgia for me. We decide to watch "Teenage Mutant Ninja Turtles 2: Secret of the Ooze" while we ate our pizza. Something about that movie gets me pumped up to fight Silas. Like we are going to be taking on the Shredder; like the turtles at the end of the movie. What can I say? I will always be a kid at heart. Marie had never seen the movie, so she couldn't understand the concept of mutant turtles knowing ninjitsu and for some reason have an enemy named shredder who had a metal hat. She was very confused by it all. She still enjoyed the movie, at least.

Now that the movie was over, I take Ginger outside to do her business. There is a doggy door to the backyard, which won't affect or trip our magical traps, fortunately. We start off by going to the front door. I bring out two water cannons and four syringes. Marie kneels down in front of them. She speaks some words; I am pretty sure is Latin. The items then float up in the air and lock into their places. It is almost as if they were hooked up to some sort of hydraulic for a show as they placed into their spots, moving robotically. Not sure if I will ever get used to something like that.

Next, we move our way to the back door. Same type of thing. All the weapons get set into their magical death dealing spots. At this point, all we have to do is wait for tomorrow. Wait for the motherfucker to come over and be dealt with. Give him the painful death he deserves after the death and destruction he delivered onto this town of mine. Also, he has done so many bad things to Marie, and who knows how many other women he has exploited. Made them marry him to be a part of the coven. Sure, the girls get immortality basically and they get these awesome magical gifts. That does not give him the right to take full advantage of them to be used for pleasure for himself. It is about time one of those exploited brings the pain back to him. I am glad that I will be there to witness and play a role in giving him what he deserves.

Now that we have armed the house, have had our fill of entertainment, and food, Marie wanted to perform a protection ritual. This will be a type of blessing, one that will hopefully protect us through the chaos tomorrow. We make our way to the Livingroom where we place a black blanket on the ground. There are symbols around in a circle. In the middle of the circle is a pentagram. This is going to be very serious.

Marie sits in the middle of the pentagram. There she has a big golden chalice, and two candle stick holders loaded with candles. She snaps her fingers and then we had light. Or, fire I guess, is more accurate. The important things right now are going to be the offerings we give to this deity. In which, I just realized that I don't know what deity it is we are even calling on. I don't even know what it is we are offering to the deity. I guess we will find out and try to work our way through this. Marie waves me over to sit next to her in the middle of the pentagram, I comply. From here, Marie stands up, looks at me and tells me, "Ok Mark, I will need you to repeat after me throughout this whole thing, ok? Those who request protection, if accepted will receive it. One cannot request for multiples at one time."

"Ok Marie, I am with you five hundred percent."

"Tonight, I will be requesting the guidance, the protection of an all-powerful deity."

"Tonight, I will be requesting the guidance, the protection of an all-powerful deity."

"Tonight, I call upon the Dark Maiden, the mother of demons. Lilith, I call upon you for protection and revenge against one who has wronged me."

"Tonight, I call upon the Dark Maiden, the mother of demons. Lilith, I call upon you for protection and revenge against one who has wronged me."

"Lilith, come forth for I shall shed my blood I shall offer some of my life force for protection. If granted, I will bring you the life of another. I will give you the soul of my wrongdoer. You shall have Silas."

"Lilith, come forth for I shall shed my blood. I shall offer some of my life force for protection. If granted, I will bring you the life of another. I will give you the soul of my wrongdoer. You shall have Silas."

After I had completed my verse, Marie took a blade, an ancient-looking blade. Ancient looking even. She sliced the wrist of her left arm and drained blood into one of the chalices. Afterwards, she spun around in a circle, in a fast movement so the blood would spray into a circular formation. She then handed me the blade and told me to do the same. I was a little reluctant at first, but I repeated the same act as her. Only, I used the other chalice for my blood. It was very important that we both used individual offerings.

Marie handed me a jar with what looked like powder in it. She said it was yarrow powder and to pack it in the cut and wrap it with the cloth she gave me. I guess that stops the bleeding fast. After doing that we both kneel in front of our blood filled chalices. I follow her lead in bowing down and putting our faces down with our arms extended out in front of us. I guess they call it child's pose in yoga.

While sitting in this position, I start to hear rustling around us. Almost as if there were hundreds of feet running around our circular blanket. This didn't make any sense to me being we were in my Livingroom. It was only us in the house, so I guess our call to Lilith is being answered. I turn my head to peak at what was going on, and I see basically a black cloud of smoke. But there were random faces in the smoke. I would see the feet at the bottom running. Some were human, many were not. The faces, were terrifying. Some looked like a regular person, others were skin melting off of them, or chunks of flesh missing. There were also faces that were animalistic, but kind of human as well. There is no way of explaining it, besides that there were demons running circles around us.

Marie quickly told me not to look, to keep

my head down until we were told to do otherwise. I could hear footsteps walking toward us now. Right in front, leading up to the chalices. It was human, barefoot, yet sounded very elegant. Then, I hear a very feminine voice, soft and sexy sounding.

"Rise my children." Lilith commanded.

I see out of the corner of my eye that Marie started to sit up onto her knees, so I followed. When I am kneeling, I look forward and see this beautiful woman standing in front of us. She is barefoot, wearing all black, sheer material. It was a skirt that went down to her knees, but there were two large slits that went all the way up to the top so her entire legs were shown. The top was just pieces of the sheer cloth wrapped around her like a small halter top. The cloth looked ragged, yet elegant. Like the frayed cloth was meant to be that way, almost Egyptian looking. She had long jet black hair, a sleek, gorgeous face. There was no color to her eyes, it was the white of her eye, and then black iris.

At this point I am in a bit of shock, here is

Lilith. The Lilith. From the bible Lilith. There is the cloud of demons running around us as well. I don't even know what to think about that. The crazy part of that, they are running so fast, but it now looks like they are moving in slow motion. Lilith looks back and forth slowly from Marie to me and back.

Lilith says, "You called upon me children. You say you need protection. You have been wronged. Who is this Silas, and what are his offenses."

Marie responds, "Yes Lilith, Silas has murdered many of innocence. In spite of us. Silas plans to take the life of my companion here tomorrow. Silas then plans to enslave me and wed him to do his every bidding. With no consent or care."

"Marie, you have converted into his coven, yes?"

"They granted me my powers; however, I did not complete the full Ritum Magni to ascend into the coven wholly."

"I see. This is your companion? Your love?

You have granted him powers, I see. You choose to bond with him in full?"

"Yes, I have bonded with him. Imprinted to him. He is I, and I is he."

"I see. This Silas, he is powerful? He is of the elders?"

"Yes, he is very old and powerful. This is why I have called on you. I believe only you can grant this kind of protection."

"I see. I am not fond of this type of man. One to want to control a woman. I will gladly grant you protection. You must complete one task in order for this to be complete. When you take his life, I need you to take his blood into this flask."

A black flask drops in front of us.

"You must fill this flask, and when you do, once complete, it will send to me. Only then will I take all of his life force. I will drain him completely and take his soul with me. You will have protection. You will still need to fight. You will need to defend yourself. He will still be able to kill you. I can only give so much protection. The elders will be able to work around that, eventually. Be wise in attack. I now accept your offering in exchange."

Lilith then drinks both chalices. As she drinks, blood spills slightly out of the corners of her mouth and the crimson liquid drips down her striking figure. She slams the chalices down, and black flames rise throughout the demon circle. I look at Marie, and she appears to be engulfed in the flame as well. I feel the surge as it flows throughout my body as well. It is incredible; it feels like bliss. A special euphoria of pleasure and peacefulness. Being blessed by a deity of that caliber is something that is unexplainably incredible.

We now have the tools that we need in order to take Silas down. He won't know what hit him. It is now time for us to lie down and get some rest. We will need every ounce of energy, every morsel in our body will need to be ready for the unforgiving combat we will be enduring tomorrow. If all works out as planned, that won't be the case. In a perfect world, Silas will walk through the door, be shot with the squirt guns, and injected by the syringes, drop to the floor. We cut his neck and drain his blood into the flask, and we all live happily ever after. Well, at least we do. Silas will be with Lilith, who I am sure has many plans of what she wants to do to his soul. I unfortunately have a feeling it won't be that easy though. I guess we will have to wait and find out.

chapter 24

oday is the day. We will fight for our lives. We will fight for many people's lives. They don't even know that this battle will happen in the midst of their town. We are doing this for us. We are doing this for them. We are doing this for the sake of all humanity. Silas must die.

Just as the start of every day, we both wake at the same time. This time, we hold each other a little longer. We embrace our warmth to one another. There is a mutual understanding; we know that it is possible this is the last time we can do this. We get up and continue on with what has become our normal morning routine. I make the coffee; Marie cooks up the breakfast for us. We sit at the table where we normally chat and figure out what we will do for the day. This time, we both just pick at our plates and barely sip our coffee. We don't have too much to say either. At this point, I think we are just hoping to survive the day and not have to suffer too much in the process.

Not knowing exactly when Silas will be coming, we are both on high alert. We basically have to stay close to where we will be stationed for the war zone. I do have cameras facing out towards the street that have motion detection. However, they go off all day because of cars driving by. For all we know, Silas might be using some sort of cloaking magic as well. I am not counting on the cameras being of any use for us.

I ask Marie, "Do you have any guess on when Silas might come to attack?"

"I have been thinking about this. Knowing him, he will want to get it done right away. He doesn't like to wait; he wants to handle his business as soon as possible. That being said, he will probably eat a meal and then come straight here. He does wake up later in the day, so if I had to guess, I would think he would be here around 2:00pm."

"Ok, well, we have a roundabout time at least. You know him best, so I would imagine you couldn't be too far off."

"Let's hope I am right."

It is now around noon. I guess it's time for us to eat lunch. Hard to even think about eating again. My stomach is in knots. But it is important that we get some food in us. I want to be at one hundred percent for this. I wanted to eat really clean for this meal as well. I decided I would heat up some nice ribeye steaks for us. Marie was putting together a superfood salad for us as well. This time, we both ate our food, and we ate it pretty fast. I don't think we realized how hungry we really were.

It was time to take Ginger outside to the do her business so I can take her upstairs and close her into the guest room. At this point it is now 1:30pm. Ginger is locked away, and we get near our positions. I am now just monitoring the outdoor camera, hoping I will see him when he starts walking up. Silas is pretty pretentious, so I wouldn't put it past him to just stroll up not being cloaked, not caring whatsoever.

It gets to be ten minutes to 2:00pm, so I decide we should take a quick pee break before it gets started. Marie runs to the bathroom and back, and then I go take my turn. As I return to my station and look at the camera, I see something off in the distance. It looks like a person walking towards my house, but they are pretty far away. They start to get closer; I can now confirm that it is indeed Silas. I knew he wouldn't care and just waltz up. I call to Marie and let her know it's about to be go time. She quickly gets to her position and cloaks herself. I tuck myself back into the room and continue to watch from the screen.

I was right; he is just walking right up to the front door. He gets to the door and stops in front of it. I see him moving his head around, as if he is cracking his neck. He looks up at the camera directly, smiles and winks. The camera goes black. The front door blasts open, and Silas comes in bearing an explosion. The super soakers blast him in the face, the syringes drop and all four sticks into his shoulders, neck and head. He screams in agony. He is flailing his arms around as if he was trying to punch the air. His eyes start to bleed. Blood is pouring out of his mouth. His skin is starting boil and blister. Parts of his flesh is even falling off. He falls to the ground face first. After about three minutes of him screaming and convulsing, it finally stops.

I come out of the room, "Marie, did he just die? Holy shit, that was easy."

"Yea, that seemed a little too easy. Let's drain his blood and get it over with."

Marie walks up to the body holding the flask and blade ready to bleed him out. I make my way over quickly; we turn him over and then I see it.

"Fuck. It's not him. That's Jim who lived

down the street." I said mortified.

Marie looks up at me and her eyes open wider than I have ever seen. Her mouth moves as if she is saying fuck, but nothing comes out. We both turn to the front door and there Silas is standing with an enormous grin.

Silas says, "What's the matter? You look like you've seen a ghost." He pauses for three seconds, then says, "Boo."

We both turn to run, but he uses his telekinetic power to throw Marie across the room into the wall. He lifts me into the air, just hovering, and makes the motion like he is flicking something with his fingers. I fly across the living room and land in the kitchen. It felt as if I was hit with a giant sledgehammer in the chest. I am on the ground, gasping for air.

Silas was walking toward me and said, "See, I told you. You should've stayed out of my business. You should've just handed her over to me. Then none of this would've had to happen. Blair would still be alive. Your entire city would still be a place. You do know that after I am done with you, I plan on bringing this whole city down."

I look for my water gun hoping that I didn t lose it in my flight, to only see that it has broken and all the liquid has drained onto the ground. As I am trying to kneel up before he gets to me, I reach into my side pant pocket and pull out the syringe. I uncap the needle, and wait till he is close enough for me to stick with it. He gets within distance and I jump up and bring the syringe down ready to stab him in the face but he freezes me again in midair. Thinking about Game of Thrones, I drop the syringe and catch it in my other hand and go to bring it up into his stomach. He releases the freeze on my body and I drop to the ground, throwing the syringe across the floor.

Silas says, "Come on, you really think that would work on me? I watched Games of Thrones too. Now what is it you have in your little syringe that you think will hurt me? I got a better idea. Let's see what happens when I inject you with it."

Silas turns around to see where it landed. I figure this is probably going to be my only chance and take the knife from my belt. I stand up and stab him right in the back. In-between his shoulder blades. Hoping I would hit his spine and paralyze him. No such luck. He hardly lets out a little shriek, as if he stubbed his toe. Looking back at me, he flicks his hand, and I get pinned against the wall. He brings up both hands in front of him and makes the motion like he is snapping a pencil in half. My index finger snaps sideways. I scream in pain. He repeats it. My middle finger snaps in the other direction. Now he brings his palm up in front of him and he runs his middle finger down the center of it and my hand splits open with a cut. It's deep, blood is pouring out of it. I don't know how much longer I can last without passing out. I realize I am about to die.

He flicks the air, which sends a powerful hit to my forehead, slamming my head into the wall.

Silas says, "Uh uh, I don't think so. I am not

done with you yet. I want to make sure you suffer for a long, long ti—."

Lightning slams into Silas, sending him across the room. This breaks his hold on me and I drop to the ground. I look up and see Marie walking toward him with her hands out and lightning is blasting from her hands. She is repeatedly hitting him; his skin is starting to smoke. Her eyes are radiating electricity out of them like she was Storm from the *X-Men*. She is walking up to him and pinning him to the ground. He is screaming in agony, finally something good to see. Sounds like music to my ears. I walk over to them so I can grab the knife to cut him and bleed him out.

I get right up to him and kneel.

I say, "Looks like we will win after all."

I lift the knife, ready to slice his throat after Marie sent the last shockwave into him. Silas smiles and laughs. Confused, I look over to Marie. She doesn't understand either, so I turn back and pull my blade to his throat. Suddenly I am hit with my front door. Yes, my front door flew across the room and smashed me against yet another wall. Marie looks back and sees Emerald. One of Silas' other wives from the coven.

Emerald smiles devilishly and says, "Did you miss me, Marie? I was really hoping you were going to join us wives. We could've had so much fun together."

She throws a knife, and it stabs right into Marie's right clavicle. Marie cries out in pain. Emerald throws another knife. This one hit Marie in her left thigh, dropping her to one knee. Emerald throws another knife; this one is barreling straight at Marie's face. In the last second Marie puts up her left hand. The blade impales her hand stopping centimeters from her nose.

I muster up the strength to push the door off of me. I stand up and stagger, but manage to throw my knife right at Emerald with my good hand. She catches it and throws it right back at me which hits me in the thigh and drops me to the ground. I am guessing she has a gift of making knives out of thin air, because she pulls out another one; from where, I don't know. She is slowly walking toward Marie, taunting her with the blade.

Emerald kneels down beside Marie and says, "I was always going to take everything away from you anyway."

There was a loud crash from upstairs. Then there was a break at the stairs. It was Ginger; she broke through the bannisters and jumped off of the stairs. Emerald, not being able to react fast enough started to turn and Ginger bit down onto her throat. Marie grabbed the knife away from her so she couldn't stab Ginger. Growling and tearing apart her throat. Thrashing her head side to side, Ginger drags Emerald's quivering body away. I look at Ginger who is now covered in blood. Funny enough, she is wagging her tail while ripping her to shreds. Good dog.

I look at Marie; she looks at me, we both look towards Silas. He was now standing. He appeared to be ok at this point now.

Silas says, "Well kids, this has been fun. But

it's time that I take what's mine. That's you Marie. You will have a lot of making up to do. You killed two wives, so you need to take the place of three total. Now, to finish this all off and burn this town to the ground."

Silas raises his arms above his head. Flames emanate out of his body. It is just an orb around his entire body, but increasing its size. Something happens. It freezes from moving any further. He looks confused. The flames retract back to his body until it disappears completely.

Silas says, "Well that's odd. I've never had a problem getting it up before."

A black cloud starts to run in through the house. Ginger whimpers and runs off outside. I recognize this, it's the demon cloud we saw when we called on Lilith. The room lights go dim. The demon cloud is circling the room as if they were running on the walls. Lilith walks into the room. Black smoke is seeping out of her skin. Silas looks petrified. I have never seen him with actual fear in his eyes.

Lilith says, "You must be the infamous Silas.

They promised me your soul. I will take it. You will be mine. For all the torture on the innocent. For all the women you have taken advantage of and enslaved. You will spend eternity suffering."

Silas frantically responds, "What? Wait, no. They lied to you. I am a strong High Priest in my coven. Who will lead them if I am gone? You can't do that to me. I am fucking Silas."

He points his hand at Lilith and shoots the flame into her torso. She looks down at it and laughs. She snaps her finger, and the flame is gone instantaneously. She points at him, and the demon cloud swarms him. First it is going around him. Then, they run through him in a figure eight formation. Blood is exploding out of every part of his body. Marie looks to Lilith and throws her the flask that was given to her. Lilith fills the flask up with his blood as it is draining from his body. Lilith then opens up her mouth, and suddenly her jaw enlarges and appears to unhinge. She has giant pointed teeth. She bites onto his neck and drops on top of him onto the ground. The demon cloud all goes into both of them until they all vanish. An apparition of Lilith appears in front of us.

Lilith says, "I have protected you. I will stop your bleeding and make sure you don't die. However, it is up to you to heal yourselves and put back together all the pieces. This Silas will be a tasty treat for a long time. His suffering will be everlasting."

Lilith disappears again for the last time.

We survived.

chapter **25**

Still lying on the floor, I look to Marie. I am still trying to comprehend the madness that ensued in my home. Realizing that the time is now 10:00 PM, I am guessing we must have passed out for a while. Marie is still just lying on the ground as well, looking around. She looks towards me and we lock eyes.

She cries a little and says, "We fucking did it Mark. We got rid of the cunt."

I chuckle, "Fuck yea. I just wish it didn't hurt

so much. You know what I just realized? We had the two other super soakers and the syringes above the back door. We could've used those. I also still have this damn machete strapped to my back. Oh well, what's done is done. All that matters is we are still here together."

"Those things dropped to the ground and broke at some point. My magical batteries, so to speak have drained out. Probably after I blasted Silas with all those lightning strikes. We are really lucky Lilith intervened. There is no way we would've survived. The other shitty part is that we won't be able to use magical healing for a quick recovery, either. We are going to have to do it the natural way. At least we have plant medicines to speed up the process."

"Fuck, I was really hoping for that magical quick fix too. Can you imagine what would've happened if Ginger didn't come blazing in to save the day too? Ginger, where are you?"

"Ginger, come here, baby."

Ginger ran in from outside, panting away. Her entire face and front body area was covered in blood. Marie was the last to call her, so she ran right up to her and started licking her face.

Marie says, "I don't even care that you are licking my face with a blood tongue. You saved my life, girl. I am forever in debt to you. You will get treats and whatever you want every day."

I respond, "Yes girl, you saved Marie. You are the goodest of all girls."

I was happy when I finally realized that when Lilith magically cauterized our wounds to stop the bleeding and such; the blades were at least removed first too. I sit up finally. Extremely dizzy, I scope out the damage of the rooms, well at least what I can see. There is blood and broken furniture, along with many other miscellaneous debris everywhere. I realize that there are no bodies left behind, at least. That's good, being we would've had to hide them the old-fashioned way. We are in no physical way to do that either.

I look down at my hand to realize that my fingers are still facing different directions, unfortunately. The cut on my palm is ok, but the fingers are still fucked.

"Hey Marie, I need you to come over here and tape up these fingers. Or do whatever it is you would do for fucked up fingers."

Marie looks at them from where she was and made a disgusted face.

"Uh, those are really bad. We can tape them to some sticks and use them as a splint. They might be messed up for a long time. Once my magical juices flow again, I can fix them. You will have that power eventually, too."

"Any idea of when it be coming back? The sooner the better."

"These things take time. I have no idea when. They need to come back naturally. Only time will tell."

Marie drags herself to her feet. She makes her way to the backyard while I just sat there patiently. I didn't really want to move my hand much, anyway. My broken fingers flopped around if I adjusted my hand slightly which was excruciating. She came back and tended to my disfigured hand. It hurt like hell, but once she set them in place and wrapped them, it wasn't too bad. They were basically in a form of a cast of a huge mixture of things with a couple of twigs surrounding them to hold them in place.

I stand up and just laugh uncontrollably.

Marie looks at me oddly and says, "You ok over there? You seem to of lost your marbles."

I respond while still laughing, "It's, ha ha, it's just that we have so much to clean up. Ha ha, we have a serious crime scene here. No magic to cover it up. Ha ha, I don't even have a front door anymore. It's hilarious."

Marie looking around, then looks back at me with a concerned look on her face. Then she erupts into laughter as well. There is so much to do, even after the atrocity we just survived. We have no energy, but need to get started right away before any police decide to take a look at why I don't have a front door.

First thing we do, is pick up the front door and place it where the opening is. The hinges are broken, and the wall is missing chunks where the screws were set. So we just gently set it in place and kind of balance it in place.

Hobbling around, we just kind of move everything into a pile in the backyard by the gate. I can just get a dumpster out here to have it all hauled away. The tricky part now will be to bleach all the floors and clean up all the blood and debris the best we can. I take Ginger out to the backyard and hose her off. I have to get Marie out to help me scrub her down to get all that blood and chunks of flesh off of her. We finally get the place to where it would at least not have any traces of death, well at least to the naked eye. It just looks like there was a demo that happened here. I can at least say I was going to redo it all if they questioned me.

The sun was coming up at this point. Exhausted, starving, and even downright delirious. We decided it was time to try to go to bed. We walk up the stairs in which I get a nice laugh when I look at the broken banister, and the thrashed guest room door. Ginger is a beast for sure. Marie and I get into the room, we take off all of our clothes and just throw them into the trash. We make our way into the bathroom so we can take a half assed shower to try to clean ourselves up so we don't stink up our bed. Finally, we make it to the bed. We don't even dry off completely. We just plop down onto the bed and pass out.

Chapter 26

Three months later. We had the downstairs remodeled. Marie has completely moved in with me. She has been making all sorts of salves, tinctures, concoctions, and whatever else to speed up our healing. We are doing pretty well at this point. Our magic has not returned yet. I have been taking this time to read the grimoires, as well as learn all the natural healing remedies. Marie is a fantastic teacher of herbal medicines. She decides she is going to open up an apothecary in town when we get back.

We are going to take a road trip with Ginger, just as we wanted to before the madness happened. We are going to hit some national parks and really immerse ourselves in nature. Marie believes we will also be recharging our magic at the same time. When we do eventually get it back, she is going to teach me how to use it. Especially use it for good. I will attempt to use the different spells and things that I have learned from the ancient grimoires. It is an incredible world we live in. What is more incredible is all that the average miss. There are so many hidden amazing things in the world. There is magic in every part of nature if you just look for it.

Before we set off, we head into town and go to the store. Luckily, the grocery store has been rebuilt and is up and running like nothing ever happened. All the townsfolk still do not know what even happened. Fortunately, that part of Marie's magic stuck and kept their minds clear of the destruction that Silas brought. For all that were killed in the store, they were just deemed as victims of the store fire and were all compensated from the insurance company.

We walk into the store and greet everyone that we see. Marie is now a part of Forestdale. She is treated as one of us. Loading up on travel foods, snacks, drinks, dog food, treats, and lots of water. It feels good knowing that my home is safe. I have found someone who is truly amazing. One thing I am not looking forward to when we get home, my mom and sister want to meet Marie. This might be more terrifying than the whole Silas debacle. They are embarrassing.

Life as I knew it is gone. Life as I now know it is becoming the norm. There is magic. I am basically immortal. There is so much more than meets the eye. I am happy that I know what I know. That I am what I now am. It is now time to embark onto a new adventure of road tripping. Most importantly, leaving this town behind for a while. I have always been here; it is time for me to explore and expand beyond my horizons. Marie has changed my life. Marie has changed this town. Nothing will ever be the same. Let's just hope there is no one else that will come looking for answers or revenge for Silas. For now, we journey. We can always handle that situation together if the inevitable happens.

The End

Also By Mike:

Short Stories: Tales of Madness

ABOUT THE AUTHOR

Michael Gregory II is the author's name at birth, but generally goes by Mike. Growing up, Mike enjoyed being a storyteller to family and friends. As a young child Mike used his mother's electric typewriter to write short stories and shared them with his grandmother. Mike started to write short stories for fun and found that it was a true passion for him. He has always loved books, movies, or even just a well-told story. Mike is enjoying this journey of sharing his passion with others.

If you would like to connect with him. You can find him on Twitter/Instagram/TikTok under the handle **@mikegreg85**. Facebook.com/mikegregory85

Website: www.mg-books.com

Please add a short review on Amazon/Goodreads and let me know what you thought of this book!

9 781088 079959